The Gorbals vampire.

Introduction;-

Extract from 1954 BBC news report;
names have been changed)

When Pc Andrew Anderson was called to Glasgow's sprawling Southern Necropolis on the evening of 23 September 1954, he expected to be dealing with a simple case of vandalism. But the bizarre sight that awaited him was to make headlines around the world and cause a moral panic that led to the introduction of strict new censorship laws in the UK.

Hundreds of children aged from four to 14, some of them armed with knives and sharpened sticks, were patrolling inside the historic graveyard. They were, they told the bemused constable, hunting a 7ft tall vampire with iron teeth who had already kidnapped and eaten two local boys.

Fear of the so-called Gorbals Vampire had spread to many of their parents, who begged Pc Anderson for assurances that there was no truth to the rumours. Newspapers at the time reported that the headmaster of a nearby primary school told everyone present that the tale was ridiculous, and police were finally able to disperse the crowd.

But the armed mob of child vampire hunters was to return immediately after sunset the following night, and the night after that. Richard Wilson, who was an eight-year-old schoolboy in the Gorbals area of the city when the vampire scare was at its height, described how Chinese whispers in the schoolyard escalated into full-blown panic. He recalled: "It all started in the playground - the word was there was a vampire and everyone was going to head out there after school.

"At three o'clock the school emptied and everyone made a beeline for it. We sat there for ages on the wall waiting and waiting. I wouldn't go in because it was a bit scary for me"

"I think somebody saw someone wandering about and the cry went up: 'There's the vampire!'

"That was it - that was the word to get off that wall quick and get away from it.

"I just remember scampering home to my mother: 'What's the matter with you?' 'I've seen a vampire!' and I got a clout round the ear for my trouble. I didn't really know what a vampire was."

There were no records of any missing children in Glasgow at the time, and media reports of the incident began to search for the origins of the urban myth that had gripped the city.

The blame was quickly laid at the door of American comic books with chilling titles such as Tales from the Crypt and The Vault of Horror, whose graphic images of terrifying monsters were becoming increasingly popular among Scottish youngsters. These comics, so the theory went, were corrupting the imaginations of children and inflaming them with fear of the unknown.

A few dissenting academics pointed out there was no mention of a creature matching the description of the Gorbals Vampire in any of these comics. There was, however, a monster with iron teeth in the Bible (Daniel 7.7) and in a poem taught in local schools. But their voices were drowned out in the media and political frenzy that was by now demanding action to be taken to prevent even more young minds from being "polluted" by the "terrifying and corrupt" comic books.

The government responded to the clamour by introducing the Children and Young Persons (Harmful Publications) Act 1955 which, for the first time, specifically banned the sale of magazines and comics portraying "incidents of a repulsive or horrible nature" to minors.

Another of those who had gathered at the graveyard as a child, Tony Malcolm, said the Necropolis provided the perfect stage for a vampire story to take root, with the noise and light from the nearby ironworks casting spooky shadows across the graves in which some 250,000 Glaswegians had been laid to rest. Mr Malcolm said it had been common for naughty children in the area to be threatened with the Iron Man - a local equivalent of the Bogeyman - by their exasperated parents.

Neither Mr Malcolm nor Mr Wilson had televisions in their homes at the time, and neither had ever seen a horror movie or read a horror comic. Comic book expert Barry Forshaw said getting their hands on one of the underground American horror comics had been like finding the Holy Grail for schoolyards of British children reared on the squeaky clean fare found every week inside the Beano and Dandy - both of which are produced in Scotland.

The story of the Gorbals Vampire had been a gift to the unlikely alliance of teachers, communists and Christians who had their own individual reasons for crusading against the corrupting influence of American comics, he said.

....
....

But maybe just maybe it wasn't a myth; maybe it was easier for everyone involved to label it a myth and an overactive imagination. You be the judge.

Chapter one; Braehead Retail Park; McDonalds; January 4th 2015.

'Here Sonny that looks like snow out there, it's cauld enough to seriously damage a brass monkey's parental possibilities' I said, stealing a chip from the cardboard packet on the table in front of him.

In case you were wondering, I am Thomas Andrew Mundell, or if you like acronyms Tam. Sonny is Alexander Thompson. We were best mates back in the day. In fact it is no exaggeration to call us the very best of mates, closer than brothers. You get that close to someone when you share a trauma or two with them. We shared more than a few, well you tend to find trauma comes calling on a regular basis when you are a Glaswegian vampire hunter.

'Maggie thinks he might be back' Sonny said spilling at least half of his strawberry milk shake down his already stained sweatshirt.

I didn't need to ask who 'he' was. He was the infamous Gorbals vampire, who some people, back in the day referred to as 'iron man'. The Iron man thing was complete rubbish that was made up by an old bible basher who used to wander around the Gorbals and Glasgow cross. Waving his battered bible in your face and screaming 'The iron man will get you, Listen to Daniel' for years people thought his name was Daniel but eventually they realised he was referring to Daniel in the bible, specifically Daniel's tale of the four beasts. But the Gorbals vampire wasn't a biblical beast. He was and maybe still is just a vampire a fairly low grade vampire at that.

The iron man legend came up back in 1954 when Maggie's mum was among the kids that went vampire hunting in the southern necropolis in the Gorbals. The rumour was that he was seven feet tall and had teeth of iron. I don't yet know if 1954 was the start or just another piece of the pattern.

Maggie also thought 'he' was back in 1994 when three weans went missing in Govan. We will come to that later because she was right that time. She also thought 'he' was back when two thirteen year old lassies went missing in Springburn in 2004. That time she was wrong the kids turned up after a couple of days, one of them was pregnant to her young cousin, which explained their panic.

So this was most probably another false alarm. Every time a wean was twenty minutes late home from school Maggie thought 'he' was back. She's never been married, our Margaret Cameron which is a shame because she was a lovely looking lassie then and is a lovely looking woman now. She might be nearly 54 now but I still would.

Theoretically I mean if I was single, which I am not. I am on my third wife now. I might have cracked it this time its lasted fifteen years which is three times what marriages one and two lasted put together. I am ages with Maggie but young at heart. Sonny is two years younger as are Stevie P and JJ. Stevie P is Steven Paterson. JJ is Janet Jackson. I know. But she was born in 1963 long before the Jackson five was famous so you canny really blame her mum and dad. She had a wee brother and I bet you canny guess his name. No you're wrong it was Thomas, the same as me. I wish it had been Michael that would have been brilliant. He was called Tommy, unlike me, everybody calls me Tam. Tam the bam when I was in my twenties and reasonably wild, and then Tam the lamb for a wee while when I kicked the fighting lark into touch.

We were the famous five, in an Enid Blyton on acid sort of way. We met up whilst we were all still in primary school, Abbotsford primary school for the three boys and St John's primary for the lassies. We were aged between eight and ten and we have been in each other's lives ever since. These days we have two major things in common us five. We are all vampire hunters (some say vampire killers) and we are all childless. All of us claim the childlessness is not deliberate even to each other. But it's not true; I for one didn't want to have children. Knowing what I know and seeing what I have seen, I couldn't have possibly ever closed my eyes and slept if I had had children. I suspect the others are the same but don't want to admit it, not even to themselves.

'Here she comes' Sonny spoke through his second chicken deluxe sandwich and nodded towards something behind me. It was Maggie mayhem. She got that nickname in primary seven and it has stuck with her ever since. She was the clumsiest person you could ever imagine meeting. If there was a rug waiting to be tripped over she found it, and tripped over it. I swear to god I saw her slip on a banana skin once, I think she might possibly be the only person in the world to have really done that. If she ever dies, because I think there is a possibility she may be immortal, I would lay a bet that it will be a piano falling out of a three storey window that kills her. That's what she's like she attracts accidents, bizarre accidents.

She was sauntering towards us head down wiping something off her skirt god knows what it was. But she was concentrating on that so missed the guy pushing his chair back and standing up to leave. She collided with the chair, somehow wrapped a leg around it and fell backwards against another table. Spilling the contents of two small children's happy meals all over the floor.

'I'm sorry, I'm sorry' she said trying to salvage what she could from the floor. She looked at the soggy and pitiful mess and smiled apologetically at the parents of the children. 'I better buy the children a new happy meal' she said still smiling her apologies.

'Aye ye better' the daddy bear growled. My ears pricked up and Sonny sat up straighter.

'Shut up you, ya hooligan' Mummy bear growled at daddy bear 'the weans were nearly finished anyway. What are you like; you would cause a row in an empty room. It's alright missus, it was an accident don't you bother your arse getting them anything else they have had enough'

She was right about that, they had had enough, both of them were seriously overweight but strangely didn't look out of place in Macdonald's, they had hardly looked up from their Iphones since I had got there. That didn't stop Maggie from handing them a two pound coin each and telling them to get some sweets. She also gave mummy bear a wee smile and daddy bear a maniacal grin that probably chilled his blood just a bit.

'Tam, Sonny' she nodded to both of us 'Where's JJ and Stevie P, we said two o'clock'

'Maggie, not everybody just drops everything when you shout you know' Sonny admonished her. 'It's only ten past two be patient'

'You do, you're always first here' she smiled at him and pushed her back behind her ears so she could kiss him on his baldy spot and pinch his jowly cheeks. Her hair was like the rest of her it looked untidy but on closer examination it was very well maintained. It was black with the merest hint of purple highlights. It had to be dyed because there wasn't a grey hair in sight. JJ teases her about it all the time. She is two years younger than Maggie and her hair is almost entirely white.

'Stevie P, texted me, he's in traffic on the M8 he will be here shortly and JJ's with him.' I said shrugging my shoulders. Stevie was always late, it was probably genetic. His old man had a job driving a hearse for a while until they sacked him for being too slow.

'Why are we meeting here again?' I asked looking round disconsolately 'Why McDonalds for god's sake. We could have just as easily met at the Brewers Fayre in Hillington or even Ikea would be better than this. I'm fifty four, he's fifty two and before you came we were sitting here like two paedo's in a pick and mix'

'Did you not say we could meet here' Maggie asked Sonny.

'No I did not are you daft. It was Stevie P' and just as we said it we heard Stevie arrive. Well we heard the squeal of his brakes as he narrowly avoided running over the big blue waste bin in the car park.

Stevie walked in with Janet, you could have been forgiven for thinking he had come in with his mum. He had on a leather jacket a *Metallica* tee shirt and a pair of hipster jeans that showed his pants when he bent over, And I almost forgot a pair of *Bvlgari* sunglasses which I am sure were for a woman. Sunglasses in January, in Scotland, mind you. He was 52 looked 42 and thought he was 32 and acted 22 at times.

Janet on the other hand was 52 looked 62 and acted 72. That's probably not fair she was a bit podgy and dressed a bit old womanish. She wasn't fat not by the standards of your average

Asda Govan shopper but she was getting there. It was her bloody hair, which she had tied back in a ponytail today that made her look old. It was steely grey and looked like it could do with a good conditioner on it; it looked like a real horse's tail rather than a ponytail. And the brown cardigan with the duffel coat fasteners didn't help make her look any younger. I looked at her and hoped if we were going vampire hunting together again, that we wouldn't have to run through the necropolis in the middle of the night like we did the last time. And there was no way I was carrying her on my back like I did in 1974after she twisted her ankle when Maggie barged into her and made her trip over a fallen gravestone.

Stevie looked round Macdonald's first before he sat down. He was a predator on the lookout for prey. He reckoned MacDonald's was a great place to meet single mums who wanted fun but not commitment. By the way before I forget to mention Stevie P, was his own idea for a nickname, apparently some football player that he thought he had an affinity with was called Stevie G. he refused to answer us for weeks unless we addressed him as Stevie P. I'm making him sound childish and vain, but that's only because he is.

'Tam the scam' he said raising a hand for a high five, I childishly indulged him.

'What are you doing ya fanny' were my first words to him. He only smiled imagining I was indulging in banter with him. I wasn't I was calling him a fanny and I meant it. He tried every time we met to call me something different but it always had to be tam the something as long as the something rhymed with Tam. He called me Tam the Cam once and when I asked him what the hell a cam was he said 'It's a river in Cambridge, I spotted it the last time I was down' He had no sensible answer when I asked him why he would call me a river in Cambridge, he just tapped his index finger on the side of his nose and said 'You know'. I'm telling you he is a fanny.

Janet prodded me in the back 'Sit down Tam the Lamb and leave him alone'. That was her favourite of all time and she refused to call me anything else. I turned round and gave her a big hug. I love hugging Janet I could stay in there for hours.

She disentangled herself from me and sat down and said 'Right Maggie hit us with it, why do you think he's back'

Maggie was taking her laptop out of its case but had somehow got the Velcro strap stuck to the sleeve of her jumper so was finding it difficult to put it on the table. Sonny helped her separate them and put the case under the table.

'Three fourteen year old lassies have turned up missing from the Gorbals over the last six weeks. Two of them went missing on Boxing Day and one of them went hasn't been seen since New Year's Day' she started as she fired up her laptop. None of us interrupted, there was no point. She had gathered us for a reason and wouldn't reveal the reason until she was ready.

'I heard about the first two from a social worker I keep in touch with. They are believed to have absconded from a children's temporary fostering facility. But Ruth, the social worker I mentioned said she knew those girls very well and they weren't typical runaways. But nobody is listening to her the girls were mature fourteen year olds and it is assumed they just got fed up being in a care home and scarpered. So that's two missing girls and nobody is looking for them. Then were another lassie who is fifteen who hasn't been seen for over a week and the police think she is probably with a boyfriend somewhere making her dad sweat it out. But the mother is hysterical she always text messages the girl twenty times a day and vice versa. But she hasn't responded to a single message since four o'clock in the morning on New Year's Day'

We waited, there was bound to be more, teenagers run away with high frequency there would be more. 'And there's this' she said, turning the laptop screen to an angle where we could all see what 'this' was.

It was an article in a Glasgow street magazine called *'The digger'*.

Who's using the Necropolis as a pet cemetery?

The Digger can report that the polis in the Gorbals are completely puggled about who might be killing cats and dogs in the Gorbals and dumping them in the Southern Necropolis. A dead bull mastiff was the first to be found it was stretched out in a cruciform manner on the plinth that covers Alexander 'Greek' Thompson's final resting place, you know the world famous architect dude. That was in August, and our man in the polis office tells us this was a big dog, man. It was drained of blood and laid out on its back, all of its legs and its back had been broken so that it could be splayed out the way it was. Our man in the polis office is nae wimp but he said it even gave him the boak.

The polis put it down to druggies; they were probably trying to have a black mass and couldn't find a virgin in the Gorbals to sacrifice. Then in September it happened again this time with a great big Rottweiler it was left on the fancy grave of Dr Nathaniel Paterson, he was a famous minister yonks ago, started the free church of Scotland supposedly, The Digger thought all churches were free but never mind. Our man in the polis office said you could have put a saddle on that Rottweiler and used it for crowd control at Parkhead. The Rottweiler had all its blood drained off the same as the mastiff but this time it had been pulverised. Our man in the polis office tells us that a vet did a post mortem and every single bone in that poor dog's body was broken. Right down to the wee bones inside its ears the vet reckoned it looked like it had been dropped out of an aeroplane and had landed on concrete and then somebody finished the job with a toffee hammer.

The polis knew what it was now; it must be a fight between drug dealers, a tit for tat kind of thing. You kill my dog and I will pulverise your dog sort of thing. That theory went boobs up in October when a cat was found skinned and drained of blood on the grave of William Cameron. I don't know why he got buried in the necropolis he was only a pawnbroker and a part time songwriter cum poet not really a high heid yin, maybe he slipped somebody a brown envelope, it has been known. Our man in the polis office said nobody even knew it was a cat at first. It was a local woman that phoned it in and didn't leave her name. When the first two polis turned up they thought it was a rabbit, apparently a skinned cat looks a bit like a rabbit, who knew.

So now the finest minds in Strathclyde Constabulary were fuddled and mucked, what sort of drug dealer would have a cat? Somebody that was dealing aspirin or lem-sips maybe? They toyed with a theory that it was weans larking about. Think on that for a minute. The top detectives at Strathclyde polis thought that the weans in the Gorbals lark about by killing eight stone terror dogs and skinning cats. Maybe back in the sixties but not now pal they wouldn't put their ipads down for long enough. The same thing happened again in November another cat, another skinned and drained cat to be precise. Apparently this was a ginger tom, now how could the vet tell that if it had been skinned, another mystery eh. This cat was hung from *the White lady*. If you don't know the story about *The White lady* it's quite interesting.

It's a monument to a carpet manufacturer's wife and her housekeeper; apparently they are both buried under it. They got killed together when they were crossing Queens's drive and got hit by a tram. What's interesting is that people say the eyes of the statue follow you around wherever you go, and the statue glows in the night. The Digger won't be checking that out but you can if you want. This time the cat was hung around *the white Lady's* neck with a bit of string. Nothing happened in December maybe the pet slayer was in a Christmassy mood. Our man in the polis office tells me that officers will be patrolling through January so watch this space muckers.

We looked at each other and then we all looked at Maggie to let her articulate what we were thinking. 'Not only is he back but he's telling us he is back he's taunting us' We automatically knew what she meant. The first grave was that of Alexander 'Greek' Thompson, we have our own Alexander 'Sonny' Thompson. The second grave was A Dr Paterson. We have our Steven Paterson who was called doc at school because of his buck teeth (What's up doc). Then there was William Cameron the pawnbroker and poet, and we had our own Maggie Cameron who was known to write the occasional stanza and coincidentally was no stranger to the pawn in the seventies. We then have *The White Lady* which could possibly be a reference to our soul sister JJ, because of her white hair. The clincher was that her first ever strand of white hair had appeared when she was ten years old and the Gorbals Vampire licked her face. I will tell you about that later.

That only left me, 'Tam the sham' Stevie P piped up 'I knew you weren't really one of us, I knew you were an impostor.

I smiled, 'Well done Stevie that was a nice one. I do feel a bit left out he could have left me some sort of present. Even if he only left me the remains of the broken baseball bat I jammed into his bloodless fuckin heart back in the day'

Janet was hyperventilating almost, Sonny was waving a newspaper in her face and Stevie was bending down talking to her calmly. Maggie and I stared at each other; we didn't have to say the words. We knew. He was back. And he wanted a rematch, well bub bring it on. Her eyes lit up with the same glow as way back then. This thing this monster, this abomination didn't scare us. We killed him once, twice before in fact we would do it again, this time for good.

Janet let out a whimper and Sonny consoled her with soothing words and sounded exactly like he did twenty years before when Janet told us about seeing her dead brother at her window.

Chapter two; Sonny's ma's house December 27th 1974.

'Tommy's missin' Janet said this in a rush as if it was one word 'Tommy'smissin, he's fucking missin' she repeated.

Stevie, Sonny and I were playing three card brag, I was winning. 'We heard you Janet, what do you mean missin?' Sonny put his cards down on the table face up. Clearly the game was over, I had been winning as well.

'He hasn't come in since last night' she said still in a panic.

'Janet calm down, is he not just at wee Brian's house, he's always round there. Brian got a chopper for his Christmas and your Tommy is never off it. Maybe he loves it so much he has run away to Gretna with it to get married.' I said to the appreciation of Stevie and Sonny, Janet not so much.

'He's really missing Tam, my ma's frantic. My da's walking the streets he's even had the caretaker at the flats looking in midden bins and all that. Tommy's a cheeky wee bastart but he wouldn't stay out all night in the winter especially with how cauld it is. There's nothing of him, he will be freezing' she said and tears were now running freely down her cheek.

I was thirteen I didn't know how to deal with a lassie greeting, I thought about punching her on the arm and telling her to shut up. But luckily Sonny was there. He put an arm around her shoulder, tried to console her and said 'Don't worry about it we will all go out and find him, he canny be that far away. If he is cycling to Gretna I doubt if he will be out of Glasgow yet, no with his wee skinny legs' Janet tried to smile but it just wouldn't form on her lips they were quivering too much.

We trooped round to her ma's house and immediately spotted her da in the next street, stopping everybody that was passing and talking to them, he looked agitated. There was a police car at Janet's close when we got there, well no really her close. It was the entrance to the block of flats on Queen Elizabeth square where she lived on the fifteenth floor. I was feart to stand at her windows without a parachute on. The four of us crowded into the lift but before the door could close Maggie skipped in beside us 'What's going down brother's' she asked, she watched far too much *Starsky and Hutch* apparently that *David Soul*, the one with blonde hair, was a dreamboat.

'Tommy'smissinandnobodycanfindhimandhecouldbedead' Janet ejaculated in a hurry.

I translated 'Her wee brother Tommy didn't come home last night and nobody knows where he is, everybody's worrying about him'

Maggie started to say something but then glanced at me and changed her mind. She gave Janet a wee cuddle and asked how her ma was coping with it. That didn't help Janet just burst into tears all over again. We got off the lift on Janet's corridor but I doubt we were going to get in her house. It was mobbed, I could see at least two of her uncles and a police woman standing at the door. One of her uncles was having a wee grab at the polis woman's bum but she didnae seem to be complaining. Most of the houses along the corridor had their doors open so I dare say the neighbours were in Janet's house too. It looked like a bit of a circus. I was half expecting a juggler or a clown to burst out on a unicycle.

'Come on we will go down to mine' Maggie said. She lived in the same block but on the third floor, if you fell out of her window you might hurt yourself bad but you wouldn't have to learn to fly.

'You go in and see your maw first Janet, she will be worrying about you now' Sonny said, as usual being the sensible one.

'Naw I canny, what if he's dead. What if that's why the polis are here. He's dead Tam isn't he?' she gasped and looked at me for an answer.

What answer could I give her, there did seem to be a lot of fuss over a ten year old boy staying out all night. Okay he was a bit young but he was probably sitting in some pal's house watching *Tiswas* or *Tom and Jerry* or something. But it was a bit weird that he hadn't surfaced yet so I gave her the most honest answer I could. 'I dunno' I said and shrugged my shoulders. It was obvious why they looked to me for leadership.

She went in reluctantly and emerged five minutes later and came down to Maggie's house in a hurry and in a bad mood 'There's no news' she said and added 'She didn't even know I had went out' Janet seemed disturbed by this, the whole block of flats were in a state of alarm about Tommy but her ma hadn't even noticed she wasn't in the house. I think she took it the wrong way, her ma had seen her this morning so she knew she was okay. She was probably being a twelve year old girl, over sensitive, precious and greeting. Sonny put his arm round her again, I don't know if he was trying to cop a feel or turning into a wee Nancy but he was starting to get on my nerves with all of the touchy feely stuff.

'Who wants tea and toast' Maggie asked everybody instantly responded 'Me'. She pulled me by the arm into the kitchen as she told the rest of them turn on the electric fire but just two bars and put the telly on. 'Come on help me Tam' she insisted.

'Go and make the toast Tam the Jam' was Stevie's contribution to the whole morning. I answered with a sardonic grin which was lost on him as he probably thought it was just a grin.

Maggie stuck four slices of toast under the grill and put the kettle on the ring, it was one of those with the wee whistle contraption on the spout.

'Is your ma at work?' I asked her, Maggie's da had died when she was about four or five. He had been stabbed to death in a gang fight at the Paisley Road Toll. Her ma had two jobs one during the day and one at night in a pub. Maggie's was always an easy place to be, it was as if it was her house since you hardly ever seen her ma.

'When is she no'?' Maggie asked but with a tinge of pride rather than resentment. She had her back to me when she asked 'Have you heard of the Gorbals vampire?' I laughed and said 'Naw, What the fuck's a Gorbals vampire?' I asked laughing, but she wasn't laughing.

'Shhh I don't want Janet to hear us. My ma was telling me about a time when she was a wee lassie maybe about ten or eleven. In 1954 there was a vampire about here and it killed and ate two local weans. It was supposed to be about seven feet tall with iron teeth. Anyway hundreds of weans went after this vampire in the Southern Necropolis and they killed it hacked it to bits so they did. My ma was there when they done it. It was all over the papers my ma's got a scrap book in her bedroom, I will show it to you later when Janet isn't here. My ma said it was all covered up, the papers all say the weans were wandering about with sharpened sticks and kitchen knives but it turned out to be a hoax. According to my ma they killed a monster and then the polis hushed it all up but she was there she saw it. Ask her'

'Is that true? Let me see the scrapbook' I asked. She went to the bedroom and came back with a co-op carrier bag with a book and some other scraps of paper in it.

'Look at it after when you get home' she advised, looked at me worriedly and said 'Tommy isn't the first wean to go missing'

'Since when?'

'My ma said a woman in her work told her that a wee brother and sister vanished out of their house in Norfolk court last week. The polis are ignoring it because the woman has fell out with her man and they think he has scarpered with them, but his brother has said he is away working in Germany and he wouldn't take the weans with him, he's no' really that interested in them at the best of times'

I looked at her and wondered if it was her that was worried or her ma, is her ma some kind of bampot maybe? I mean really a Gorbals Vampire. The only type of Vampire I knew about here were the moneylenders they would suck you dry all right and when they had sucked all your money then they might well start on your blood, the bastards.

'Come up to mine later on tonight and we can look through this' I said and held the bag up 'but don't mention it to them three ben there until we get a chance to look at it okay?' She nodded her acceptance and her green eyes looked full of fear, I wanted to hug her to reassure her but I didn't because I wasn't intending turning into a Nancy boy like Sonny, and trying to cop a feel from Maggie was a more dangerous game than I liked to play.

As it turned out Sonny was also with us when we finally examined the scrapbook. He had come up to mine for no particular reason and I couldn't think of a good enough reason to not tell him what Maggie had told me. Sonny was a smart cookie, not necessarily with maths and chemistry and all that school stuff but he knew what was right and what was wrong.

'Tam this isn't likely is it? We would have heard about it, our ma's and da's would have talked about it, would they no" he asked when I told him the tale Maggie had told me. We hadn't yet looked through the scrapbook we were waiting for Maggie. But then decided why wait she had seen it all before. So we started looking and we found a load of old newspaper cuttings from everywhere, not just Glasgow. There was one from time magazine in America another one from Australia. There were also a few ring-bound notebooks the first one had doodles all over the front cover of graves and tombstones. Another one had drawings of skulls, all of the doodles and drawings were done with black ink, the drawings had almost cut through the pages, and they had been scrawled on with such force.

'Somebody looks as if they were having a bad day' I said pointing at the cover which had almost been scratched through. 'And look at this' I added as I handed a clipping to Sonny.

Sunday mail 26th September

SUNDAY MAIL, Page 3
September 26, 1954

VAMPIRE WITH IRON TEETH IS "DEAD"

THE vampire with iron teeth is dead. The vampire—which was supposed to be running amok in Glasgow's Southern Necropolis on Thursday after devouring two little boys—started children armed with penknives, sticks, and stones on a mammoth hunt.

They swarmed over the seven-foot-high wall and started searching the cemetery. The rumours swept through the Hutchesontown district of Glasgow with amazing speed. Police were called out.

Lurid comics and a horror film are blamed with starting the scare.

But last night all was quiet at the necropolis. Youngsters who swarmed the surrounding streets guiltily laughed at the idea of a vampire.

That was stuck in the first page of a notebook and somebody had scribbled along the bottom of this, *'they weren't guiltily laughing about thinking there was a vampire, they were guiltily laughing at killing a vampire'*

I turned the page and started reading more;

That policeman was too late; by the time he had turned up we had killed the beast. All he seen was us walking away from the stone grave we had dumped the vampire in. I don't know where the rubbish about a seven foot man with iron teeth came from because the thing we killed and cut into pieces was about the size of my uncle john and he's not even six feet. It was Antonio Conti that struck the final blow and no wonder. It was supposed to be his wee sister that got ate by the monster, except it didnae eat her she was lying dead at the bottom of the stone grave where we killed it.

She was lying there with no clothes on and she looked like a wee white china doll. Sandra Torrance wanted to pick her up and take her home, Tony (Antonio that is but everybody called him Tony) said no it would kill his ma. His ma was Italian she had been here since just after the war. Her man had been taken prisoner and she came over here to get him and they just stayed. Tony talked more Glaswegian than I did. His ma and da were quite old she was over forty when his wee sister was born.

So we left her and there was another wean underneath her we never seen him at first he must have been only about one or something. Johnco Murray said he had heard a woman in Queen Elizabeth square had been sent to jail because somebody said they seen her throwing her baby in the Clyde. She screamed and shouted that somebody had stolen her wean but they jailed her anyway.

Tony and Johnco cornered this thing in the far corner it was spitting and squealing because when we first seen it a big boy who I don't know stabbed it right through the heart with a big clothes pole he had sharpened. It didnae see him coming because it was concentrating on all the weans in front of it waving knives and sticks at it and he sneaked up behind it and ran it through with the big pole which this thing broke off at the front and back but there was still a bit stuck in it.

It was screeching at Johnco, he had a brush handle with a knife held on the end of it with string and he was jabbing the knife at it, the thing seemed to be getting weaker. Johnco took a wild swing at it and cut its face right open. I was close enough to see the knife slice through its cheek and there was no blood not a single drop. But that was it, Johnco slashing its face started a free for all and everybody just piled in with sticks stones and knives. Everybody took a step back after a minute or two and the thing was crouched right next to the stone coffin thing and still whimpering slightly.

I could see some of its fingers lying on the ground beside it and what looked like an ear but it could have been a bit of his cheek or arm or anything. There were lots of bits of him lying there but he was still wheezing and alive. Tony took a straight razor out of his inside jacket pocket and slashed this things throat; the cut was good and deep. The monsters head fell backwards exposing a torn throat, its head was only hanging on by the skin at the back of its neck. And yet there was still no blood I couldn't understand that, but it meant we were right all along it wisnae human it couldn't be. It was some kind of a monster I don't know if it was an actual vampire but it wisnae human. Isobel McCafferty told me she felt guilty about that night years later I told her I didn't because that thing was from hell and we sent it back. Nearly everybody ran away at that point, I didnae I stood and watched it die and the boys hack it to pieces. I wanted to make sure I saw it die.

Remind me not to get on the wrong side of Maggie's ma. I felt a bit guilty reading this stuff because I thought there was a fair chance that Maggie's ma and her pals probably killed some harmless old guy. Because let's face it vampires aren't real, Christopher lee and Peter Cushing aren't from the Gorbals.

Maggie arrived just as I was putting her ma's stuff back in the carrier bag. I looked at her with guilt all over my face. 'Do you think my ma's a murderer?' she asked me.

Why were lassies asking me such ridiculously difficult questions today I answered it as well as I could 'I dunno' I said decisively.

'I don't Tam. I think she helped to kill a monster, even if it was a human monster there were two wee babies lying at the bottom of the stone coffin it was living in' She said with desperation.

'What stone coffin. I never read anything about it living in a stone coffin' I said.

'Well you didnae read it all then. My ma was told that some of the people that were there when it got killed had actually chased it into a stone coffin the night before. But no matter how hard they tried they couldn't get the stone lid off. So they waited all day and as soon as it got dark the thing came out. That's when they killed it and they scraped all the bits of it up and put them back in there and between about thirty and forty of them managed to slide the lid across. That's why the polis never found anything when he got there except two hunner weans with sticks and knives. If he had been half an hour earlier he could have joined in my ma said.

'If the polis get a hold of that plastic bag, your maw could be in a shit load of trouble. Not to mention all the people she grasses up as well in her wee notebooks. The Italian guy for a start he cut the guy's head off for fucks sake' I said with awe.

Maggie looked at me unhappily for using the 'F' word as she called it. She hated it and was forever telling me it showed a lack of vocabulary and made me sound common. Aye right I'm from the Gorbals for flip sake; I'm never going to sound anything other than common.

'The Italian guy went to Italy to live ten years ago, his mum and dad died and he said there was nothing left here for him. He didnae even talk Italian either, imagine that going all that way home and no' being able to talk to anybody, that's a shame intit?' She said.

'Are any of the rest of them still about?' Sonny asked, not very sympathetic to the Italian murderer's plight 'Maybe we could ask some of them what happened, get a second opinion sort of thing. It was his first words since Maggie had arrived and as usual they were practical and sensible, he must get fed up being perfect all the time.

Our discussion was broken up by Stevie P shouting through the letter box. 'I'm here to see Tam the ram. Put Maggie down and open this door' he wasn't so proud of his wee joke when my ma opened the door to him and said 'What did you just say' he went as red as a sunburnt beetroot and started stammering. My ma let him down gently and told him we were in my room and to just come in but mind his language in future.

'All the street lights are off' he announced 'It's darker than a nig nogs arsehole out there'

I looked over his shoulder and said 'No we don't need anything ma, we're alright' the tube went as white as a ghost and turned round with his hands up at his face, as if my ma might slap him one. She wouldn't but I might.

'So what's the score on the door with wee Tommy, has he turned up alive yet?' he asked Maggie.

'I haven't heard a thing' she said 'and I haven't seen Janet since I left you'se lot at four o'clock'

Maybe we were about to find out because the door got chapped again and I heard my ma say 'they are in the room hen, has your wee brother turned up yet?' Janet mumbled something which must have been negative because my ma said 'Och your Tommy's always been a bit of a rascal, he'll turn up hen, mark my words it won't be long till you see him' I heard the living room door shut and my ma turning the telly up. I swear she was getting deaf; all I could hear was that crappy music from *'Are you being served'* she laughed like a nut-job at that programme and it was utter pish as well. Janet seemed to be taking her time to come into the room.

She came in and stood at the door twisting the sleeve of her cardigan between her hands one inside the cardigan and one outside. She looked at us with pure fear on her face and said 'I've seen Tommy' and burst into tears.

Maggie jumped up and started to comfort her and get her to stop greeting she was near hysterical. I was a bit surprised Sonny didn't push Maggie out of the way to get in there first. Stevie and me just looked at each other not knowing what to do.

Stevie recovered his voice before me but maybe forgot to think first before he said 'Is he dead' I slapped him on the back of his head.

'What' he said 'Look at her, if she seen him playing football in the corridor she wouldn't be like that would she, there's snotters running down her chin'

Maggie looked at Stevie in a way I never want her to look at me, he withered under her glare. 'How's it my fault now? He whined.

Maggie ushered Janet out and we could hear them going into the toilet together. Sonny looked at me, I shrugged my shoulders 'Don't fuckin ask me' I said looking over my shoulder to make sure Maggie hadn't heard me. The three of us just sat there waiting, we never said another word to each other for the ten minutes that Janet and Maggie were in the toilet. Stevie's attention was wavering by that time and he had taken a set of poker dice out of his pocket and was playing with them by himself. Just as I thought about sitting on the floor beside him Maggie led Janet back in and sat her on the edge of my bed. She smoothed out the candlewick cover first because it had become a bit ruffled.

My room was tiny, if you can imagine a prison cell with blue wallpaper a bed with a mattress covered with a candlewick, one pillow, and a tallboy with five drawers in it. Then that was it, there was a lamp on the tallboy as well so as I could read at night. All of my clothes were in the top four drawers and a spare sheet and blanket were in the bottom. The spare blanket would probably go on shortly, it was nearly January and it was freezing in this room all the time, never mind January. I normally slept with most of my clothes on anyway. In fact fairly regularly there was as much ice on the inside of my window as on the outside.

I moved onto the floor beside Stevie, Janet sat on the edge of my bed in the middle of Sonny and Maggie, she was still weeping but not hysterically, in fact it was almost silent.

'Where did you see him' I whispered as gently as I could, it was obvious he must be dead. So I was thinking she had seen his body somewhere, Sonny later told me that he had thought exactly the same thing.

Janet looked at Maggie unable to speak, Maggie spoke for her 'He was at her bedroom window'

Stevie just can't ever keep his mouth shut 'how did you no' let him in?' he asked.

This time I answered for Janet 'She lives on the fifteenth floor ya eejit'

Chapter three; Stevie P's flat, Walmer Crescent January 6th 2015

Maggie had sent us away from McDonald's at *Braehead* with tasks for all of us and an instruction to meet at Stevie's place in two days. I never minded any excuse to visit Stevie's flat. It was in Walmer crescent just off the Paisley Road West at Cessnock Street. It was a hidden gem of a wee street. Apparently it had been designed by Alexander 'Greek' Thompson, another coincidence to add to the ever growing list. It is a curved row of beautiful sandstone tenements and the only reason that the houses didn't cost a fortune was that it was hidden behind a row of grubby shops. Stevie's flat was in a five bedroom house which had been converted into two flats. Stevie's was the bigger of the two it had a bedroom a kitchen cum living room and a huge bathroom which had a scroll top bath and a walk in state of the art power shower.

Sonny and I visited him the night after he had moved in a few months before and were amazed at how stunning it was, not just the high ceilings with glorious cornices but what he had done to it.

He had two 60" televisions side by side on the main wall above a nineteenth century iron fireplace scrubbed back to its original black colour. No cabling was visible anywhere but one television was connected to an unseen *Sky Television* box and the other to an unseen computer.

The kitchen end of the large front room was fitted out like a 1950's American diner complete with chrome top bar stools and a genuine soda fountain, which had been converted to serve lager. He had two leather two seater sofa's on the wall opposite the TV wall and between the sofas and the televisions he had a dining table surrounded by six chairs. The top of the dining table was black ash wood almost six inches thick, the chairs were amazing they were made of a black plastic which you would have sworn was glass. But the clincher was that if you turned over the top of the dining table there was an air hockey table built into it.

When we saw the water bed in his bedroom and noticed it seemed to be almost the same size as the room, all we could do was laugh. 'Stevie son with the money you have spent in this flat you could have bought a time machine and just went back to the Seventy's you fanny' I suggested.

Sonny joined in the laughter but it didn't stop him collapsing backwards on to the water bed with a whoop of joy. 'If I had a girlfriend I would bring her here and pap you out Stevie' he said as he sank into the bed.

Neither Stevie nor I said anything, to our knowledge Sonny hadn't been with a woman since his wife Sylvia had died four years previously. She had committed suicide. Pills, booze, hot bath, razor blade. She had been battling depression for the previous sixteen years. Since 1994 and our previous battle with our current adversary to be exact. But that struggle against depression and her three previous attempts to take her own life didn't lessen the devastation that Sonny felt, that we all felt. But obviously not to the depth he did. Both Stevie and I spent the six months after her death helping Sonny to drink himself into oblivion, particularly when he told us the real reason behind her sixteen year depression and her suicide. It had cost him his job, his house and almost his sanity. The drinking binge had almost cost me my job and my marriage. Maggie and Janet had been there frequently pleading with us and begging us to stop and think but we couldn't. To think was to cry and to cry was to concede defeat. We had to drink until we could make the world feel okay again or die trying.

It was Sonny who eventually got us off our increasing spiral into madness and alcoholism. He met a priest who talked him down. Sonny was a protestant growing up and an agnostic as an adult. He had left Stevie and I sitting in a pub in the west end and had gone for a walk promising us he would be no more than half an hour, he needed to clear his head. He was an hour and a half and he came back sober.

'Come on guys let's kick this shite into touch, Sylvia is dead I can't undo it' he said.

He was sleeping in my back bedroom at the time, much to the displeasure of June my eminently sensible, loving and endlessly forgiving wife.

'Tell June I will be out by Friday and that I appreciate it. Why she puts up with you or me is beyond me. Tell her I love her and I'm sorry for all the shit I have put you two through and that I will be gone by Friday, deffo' he said with his normal certainty.

He was indeed out by Friday. He rented himself a bedsit flat in Albert drive in Pollokshields on the south side of Glasgow. It wasn't much to look at but it was cheap and available. His wife had been insured albeit not for a great deal of money but after six months of heavy drinking and no salary coming in he was starting to feel the pinch. A week later he had a job selling caravans. He knew nothing about selling caravans but that didn't stop him. Six months later he owned a shop on Great Western road selling caravan and camping accessories. He hadn't mentioned his wife nor had he mentioned any woman or any interest in women in general since the night he had found Sylvia dead. We were glad he had stopped drinking but despite the fact he was, on the surface at least, making a real go at re-joining life, there was no conviction in him. He appeared to be going through the motions and waiting for life to grab him rather than him grabbing it.

I was first to arrive at Stevie's, I was usually the first to arrive anywhere, except for the occasions where sonny thought he would prove that I wasn't always first by turning up two hours earlier than we had arranged to meet. Stevie wasn't in; I reached above his door where there was a ledge and a small window to let light into his hall. He stupidly left a key on this ledge for any of us to use when we needed it and to let himself in on the occasions where he lost his key or had it stolen. Stevie was a mugger and nut case magnet, I have no clue why but he got mugged at least twice a year and hooked up with nut jobs on an even more regular basis.

The key wasn't there so I sat on the bottom step opposite his flat door and settled in for a wait. The key wasn't there but there was a distinct smell of garlic on my hands Stevie must have drenched the frame of his dour with pureed garlic. I didn't smile nor did I blame him I made a mental note to do the same thing.

I wouldn't have minded a cushion or even a newspaper, concrete steps are bloody cold to sit on in Glasgow in January and my ma once told me sitting on cold stone gave you piles, and I didn't need piles thanks very much.

I was waiting less than ten minutes when Stevie's immediate neighbour appeared. She was a twenty something stunner of a nurse who knew it and played it for all it was worth.

'He's no' been in since yesterday Tam' she informed me. I knew her name Stevie had introduced me more than once. But could I bloody remember it at that moment, could I fuck. Alzheimer's flashed through my mind like it always did whenever I forgot something, Even though I am only fifty three, June tells me it's another symptom of man flu. Despite hesitating for time I still couldn't remember this lassie's name, so I tried to catch a sneaky look at the name badge on her chest. She wrapped her coat around her and gave me a look normally reserved for perverts.

'I was looking at your badge hen I couldn'y remember your name I wisnae looking at your ... anything else' I said and then wished I hadn't. That's another thing, since I had turned fifty I was finding it harder to shut the fuck up. My mouth just rattled away sometimes and kept digging and digging, why did it do that?

'Aye well you shouldn't be looking at things you canny afford anyway' she said letting her coat slide open again. 'Chantelle Fitzpatrick' it said on her badge, which was appropriate since that was her name, I remembered.

'Did he say where he was going?' I asked and then heard the close door slam and running footsteps on the stairs coming up towards us. She didn't have to answer me it was Stevie making all the noise and was breathing heavily as he reached us. He patted me on the shoulder and gave Chantelle a hug and said 'If it isnae my wee bed bath buddy, have you changed your mind about sleeping with old men yet?'

She looked at him seriously and replied 'Naw, I'm still gonny keep doing it, but you've still got no chance until you cut down on eating that raw garlic' and cackled a laugh that I had forgotten she had. OMG when god gave her the great boobs the great arse and the lovely face it must have been to compensate for that laugh. It was hideous you couldn't listen to that without wanting to put a pillow over her face. Stevie clearly thought the same because he had his door open and was pulling me in before I even had time to stick my fingers in my ears. He did stink profusely of garlic and I noticed he had a fine gold chain round his neck, I could imagine what dangled at the end of it. My crucifix was in my pocket, it was too big for a chain round my neck.

'Omfg' he said 'what a waste of a beautiful lassie, you just couldn't sleep with her could you. You would be forever just waiting for that laughing to start; it would be bound to put you off. Although I suppose you could gag her'

I didn't get a chance to answer him, Janet and Sonny walked straight in without even knocking. Janet with a few Asda bags packed with grub and Sonny with a smile I hadn't seen in some time.

'Who have you been shagging' Stevie asked him and Sonny shot him an extremely dirty look.

'What's that look for, it's obvious you're back in the game so answer the question' I said to him, backing Stevie, the grin on Sonny's face looked permanent and could only have had one cause.

Sonny glanced at Janet; she said 'Tell them, it's no' a secret Sonny for gods sake'

'Well the thing is, it's like this, the truth of the matter is, I meant to say something, I should have said something, the thing is, it's like this' he stammered.

'Aw for Christ's sake Sonny' Janet said turning to us 'It's me he's shagging now get your laughing over and done with and let me through to the kitchen these bags are breaking my arms'

I looked at Sonny he looked shyly away, 'Sonny your fifty fuckin one not twelve. Stop grinning' I said and fist pumped him while Janet's back was turned. Stevie high fived him, apparently nobody had told Stevie that high fives were out and fist pumps were in. if you could make the sound of a mini explosion as you took your fist away in slow motion that was even cooler. June had mentioned to me before that, like most things it wasn't so cool when a fifty three year old guy with a beer gut did it. I ignored her she wasn't *always* right.

Looking down at my beer gut and Sonny's and as sorry to say it as I is, even more so Janet's middle age spread. I wasn't sure we were up to vampire hunting. Stevie would be fine it seems that a diet of champagne and cocaine keeps you thin. He had eased off on the drugs recently but he seemed to have one of those metabolisms that burned whatever you threw at it. I was carrying the last ten year's *Budweiser's and Carlings* with me wherever I went, and not in a six pack. He had the same shape and build as he did when he was nineteen and a budding songwriter.

He had in fact written a handful of hit songs in the eighties. The royalties from them still provided a decent level of income, hence the fancy décor and kit in the flat.

I glanced again at Janet and remembered her as the twelve year old skinny wee girl that I carried from a graveyard with a vampire chasing me. I imagined trying to do that now. 'What are you smiling at' Janet asked me 'Sonny and me will be good, it's the right time for us'

I looked again at her and saw the real Janet. Sure she was a couple of stone heavier than she wanted to be. When she shook her hips now it took longer for them to stop shaking than she was entirely comfortable with. She was a middle aged woman and we were middle aged men, physically at least. But I saw past her bingo wings and her chubby ankles into her heart. She was still that brave and gallus and defiant twelve year old girl with her arms round my neck and her breath on my cheek as she whispered 'Run Tam run faster, it's not going to get us. Not today Tam, it's an ugly bastard and we are going to do it in' she finished with a peck on my cheek and a smile to gladden my heart which made my feet go faster until I felt as if I was flying on the wind.

'I am smiling at the two of you in fact for the two of you. It's the worst kept secret in the Glasgow you two should have got together years ago. He needs somebody to look after and so do you. It's about time.' I hugged her and whispered in her ear 'Does this mean I'm bombed out again then' and squeezed both of her arse cheeks.

She pushed me away laughing 'You had your chance, it was you that knocked me back remember' she was laughing but there seemed to be an undercurrent of regret. I hope so, I regretted in a way never becoming romantically involved with Janet or Maggie. I fantasised about both of them enough through my teenage years. They were both frequent visitors to my dream factory. But anytime a 'moment' had come along it just hadn't felt right. What we went through was too intense too surreal it would have dominated every waking thought if we had coupled up. I knew what Janet meant when she said the time was right for her and Sonny. This was the last time we could do this, we couldn't be vampire hunters into our sixties that would be ridiculous even more ridiculous than it was right now and that was bad enough. If Maggie was right and the Gorbals Vampire was back again we would need to finish it for good or die trying

It was Maggie that broke me out of my memories. She arrived in her usual whirlwind of flapping coats and hugs and kisses. She got the news from Janet about her and Sonny and said much the same as Janet had 'it's the right time' she glanced at me as she said it. I got a little jolt, I absolutely clearly in my head heard her say 'Is it the right time for us yet Tam?' It was as if she said it out loud, I looked at Sonny to see if he had heard it as well, or Stevie or Janet. None of them had just me. So I put it down to an overactive imagination, given what I had been doing for two days it was no wonder.

'Right everybody, get your coffee in your hand and dig in to the sandwiches and sausage rolls, Janet has been busy putting together while you three dinosaurs have been scratching your arses and thinking about ball games or scratching your balls and thinking about arses. And when you have filled your ample bellies then it's time to find out if we are back in the vampire killing business' Maggie announced picking up and nibbling at a tuna and sweetcorn wrap.

We sat for twenty minutes with talking about the weather and our various aches and pains, it wouldn't be long before we were talking about our medication and whose funeral was coming up like some old pensioners do, but the small talk couldn't last, and we knew what we were here for.

'Me first then I suppose' I said 'there's not a lot to report but it doesn't look good. I went to the Cardonald cat and dog home. Supposedly looking for fluffy my daughter's ginger cat. I told the lassie I was from the Gorbals and that was enough to get her started. She couldn't wait to tell me that she had at least a hundred and fifty people from the Gorbals in the last six months in looking for cats and dogs that were lost. At first she thought it must be somebody stealing them and selling them, but it was all types of mongrels and moggies, not sellable dogs like Rottweiler's or pit bulls' I finished off my part of our fact finding mission by telling them it seemed to me that something was killing pets in the Gorbals and had been doing so for the last six months.

I asked the girl if the police or the press had shown any interest and she shook her head 'It's mongrels in the Gorbals not poodles in Bearsden, why would they?'

We more or less agreed that it was a bad sign, a sign we had seen before back in 1994. It appeared likely that our adversary, whom the press had christened the Gorbals vampire back in 1954 slept for periods of around twenty years after being 'killed' And when he woke up he did so in a weak state and gathered his strength by ritualistically slaughtering small animals gaining sustenance from their blood and agony. He then progressed by snatching babies and children wherever he could and eventually built up enough strength to go after full grown adults.

Janet started with her news which could be incredible if it was true. She had posed as a freelance writer and visited various cemeteries in and around the Gorbals, She told the cemetery managers and grave diggers that she was doing a story on vandalism for a magazine and was after any recent stories about graves being desecrated or destroyed. We were aware as are most people thanks to Hollywood's obsession with them that vampires need somewhere to rest during daylight hours and that they favoured desecrated graves or tombs.

One of the grave diggers put her in touch with 'The *southern Necropolis Action group'* They were a voluntary group set up to clear all the headstones and monuments of overgrown ivy and super-size weeds, according to them Glaswegian weeds were harder to get rid of than teenage acne and what's more they keep coming back. It was mostly local people taking a pride in their area. One of the women volunteers, Agnes Lawrence, agreed to meet Janet along the road from the Southern Necropolis in the Glasgow Forge shopping centre for a coffee and tell her all about the goings on that had been reported in that *'Digger magazine'* She confessed to Janet that she had been the anonymous woman who had found the skinned cat. She had declined to leave her name because she visited the necropolis every day picking up wind-blown litter and discarded condoms and didn't want any weirdo to latch on to her. Janet told us this wee woman was five foot one tall and five foot two wide, and Janet laughed at the thought of anybody intimidating her.

When she felt a bit more comfortable with Janet it was her that brought up the subject of the Gorbals vampire. Agnes was 71 years young and had lived in the Gorbals her whole life she had been in the crowd that, according to Maggie's ma, had killed the vampire in 1954. She couldn't corroborate the story from Maggie's ma but she did say she was at the back of the crowd and that there was a lot of commotion at the front of the crowd and then they all scattered, and she bumped into the lone policeman as they all ran helter skelter to get out of there.

That wasn't the end of Mrs Lawrence's tale, Janet then recounted the next part of the conversation. 'My ma told me all about the time before' Mrs Lawrence dropped into the conversation with no preamble.

'What time before?' Janet asked her with trepidation.

'In 1934 or 1935 she wisnae sure, something was killing weans and draining them of blood in the houses around Crown street and a few of the local men including Agnes' grandfather had managed to run it off. Some people including Agnes' granny insisted that they didn't run it off they killed it and threw it off the Albert Bridge into the Clyde is what they really did. There was a lot of talk of forty weans or more dying at its hand but there was that much consumption and stuff at that time that maybe it was difficult to tell what had made a wean die. And nobody really cared about keeping records'

'I wish I could have spoken to your ma that would have been an incredible story to listen to' Janet said with a gentle smile.

'How can you no'?' Agnes asked her with a puzzled expression. 'Oh I see you think because I'm an auld fogey that she must be deid, well she isnae hen and neither is my da. They live together in an old folks home along in Brand Street in Govan. He's a bit doolally at times but at other times he's all there and a bit mair. I go and see them every couple of days I am going on Monday if you want to come along you can. They would be fair excited talking to a writer; god knows they get bored with me now after ten minutes. How much can I really have to talk about when I see them every second or third day? What did you say you were doing is it a book?'

Janet smiled and said 'No it's just a wee magazine piece but you never know. I would love to come along on Monday would it be alright if I recorded what we talk about so that I can run it past my editor?'

Mrs Lawrence agreed, Janet thought she would have agreed to virtually anything, this was probably the most exciting thing to happen to her in years. This was Sunday so the arranged visit was scheduled to take place the next day. We discussed whether Maggie or I should go with Janet but decided it would maybe be too excitement and too much for the old dears. And anyway I think maybe Janet was unhappy and found it a wee bit condescending of us to think that she couldn't handle it on her own.

'Are you two thinking I canny handle this by myself? Is that no just a bit condescending? Who died and made you two Holmes and Watson anyway?' she asked us; see I told you she wasn't happy.

Stevie was next to report his task was to find out if there had been an increase in missing persons reported or teenage runaways, or an increase in vagrants being found dead. He had a couple of pals who were ex-policeman who were now in the security business but still kept their ears to the ground. Amazingly enough one of those pals had jailed Stevie back in the nineties for possession of a class A drug. It was in fact Heroin. Stevie to this day swears it belonged to a woman he was seeing. The judge didn't believe him and gave him ninety days.

For the next six months Stevie refused to shut up about being hardened by his experience.

'It's changed me' he would say 'I no longer have as much compassion for my fellow man. I have seen the depraved levels that humanity can sink to' these depraved levels turned out to be some old con stealing his quarter ounce of Old Holborn tobacco.

He still to this day which is almost twenty years later tells people that he just met that he is a reformed criminal that has done time, But is now rehabilitated and owes society nothing, he did the crime and did the time. Sometimes I wonder why I still like him, he is such a fanny.

Stevie was hesitant when he started to speak 'I haven't heard a great deal but I hope what I did hear isn't true' He took a drag on his electronic cigarette. I suppressed a giggle, Stevie P the great rock and roller with an e-fag. You couldn't make it up.

'Apart from the three lassies Maggie mentioned on Friday the polis have only one open missing persons case and that's for a mother and her two year old baby. Apparently the last time she was seen before she vanished was walking into Riddrie cemetery. The lassie's man has a wee bit of history of lifting his hands so the polis have him in the frame for doing her in and probably the wean as well. They have interviewed him twice and he keeps screaming at them that he seen her go into the cemetery but when he ran to catch up with her she was nowhere to be seen' he paused to allow us to imagine the scene

'Anyway the polis are taking a cadaver dog team and they are going round this guy's gaff during the week to see what's what. But that's no' the worst of it, I went down the Hamish Allan centre and looked wee Sinead up'

We all looked at him warily, Sinead was an ex-girlfriend of Stevie and the two of them together were an exceptionally volatile mix. She was a thirty eight year old Irish born social worker who was forever on the verge of some kind of breakdown. When that was put together with Stevie's insecurities and puggled head there were always fireworks. The last time they broke up was because she had stabbed him in the arse with an eye pencil. He needed a tetanus jab she had pushed it in so far. Luckily it didn't break his spirit he went home with the nurse who gave him the jab.

'She is still there, by the way. The thing is she reckons that seven of her clients alone have buggered off since September. Don't get me wrong she has forty two clients on the go at any one time, but she still reckoned misplacing seven in three months was excessively careless. She had a word with some of her colleagues and the pattern was repeated they had all lost a lot more than they normally would, especially in the winter'

Maggie interceded 'Much as it worries me to say this Stevie, you need to go back and see Sinead and her colleagues, build some sort of profile of who is missing, see if there are any similarities or patterns.'

'Sonny you're up, what's on the net big boy' Maggie said as she rose and asked if everyone could use more coffee. This looked like being a late one so the general answer was yea.

Sonny lifted his lap-top on to the dining table and said 'I will send you all a pdf with the details but the main thing is that there is no real sign of this guy on social media. There's a bit of tweeting about the dead animals in the Necropolis and a bit about the wee lassies who are missing but nobody is connecting them there hasn't been a single mention of the Gorbals Vampire anywhere'

'Should we mention him them, get it out there and have everybody looking for him?' Janet asked and looked around the table.

I answered first 'I don't think so, nowadays he would be treated like a celebrity and he would get a spot on *'The riverside show'* or his own column in *'The Daily Record'*

Maggie was second to answer as she placed the coffee pot and a plate of chocolate digestives on the table 'No way, look at what happened in 1994 when we went to the police and involved that poor sergeant.

Chapter four Orkney street police station Govan 28th December 1994

He was back and he had reached the stage of targeting adults, we had discovered he was back because he had gone after Janet. Our suspicions were raised by a story on Reporting Scotland of several horses being mutilated in fields in and around Glasgow. Some bored reporter had linked this to both vampire bats attacking horses in Peru and a vampire tale from an eastern European country and suddenly vampires were in the news again. Teenage girls and older women who should know better started reporting dark strangers with accents accosting them in the alleyways of the city centre. Which was entirely possible but much more likely to be Italian sailors than our vampire.

Like most news stories it fizzled out quickly when more serious matters grabbed the headlines, like the gulf war. But it did put us on alert, which was why Janet was wearing a crucifix when she was lying on the living room floor in her flat in watching the movie *Bram Stokers Dracula, starring Winona Ryder* With her then boyfriend Liam whom she had been going out with for less than a month. She had been dozing off as much as she had been watching it, when you had seen and experienced the horrors that she had, movies weren't nearly as frightening.

She must have dozed off again because Liam was down on the floor with her now, he had been sitting on the couch and she had been lying with a cushion across his feet watching the film. But he must be getting a wee bit amorous because he was right up behind her now and she felt him lean in and bizarrely lick the side of her face from chin to eyebrow, which felt wrong. She stiffened and tried to turn her head but Liam gripped her neck quite tightly, she thought 'this isn't funny' and was about to tell him so when she seen him walk across the living room door and begin to climb the stairs announcing as he went 'Going for a razz' back in a minute.

She struggled again and whatever was behind her licked her again but this time it laughed softly as it did and said 'Hello Janet, have you missed me' She struggled violently which dislodged her crucifix from where it had been trapped between her breasts. It swung round and touched the hand that was holding her neck in a vice like grip. She heard a squeal and a hiss and was thrown across the room to land with her back against the living room door which she had closed by banging against it.

The Gorbals vampire stared at her its facial features were fading in and out between a handsome young man and the face she remembered from 1974. That of a hairless rat with pronounced molars dripping with blood.

It shifted nearer to the window smiling as it went 'I've missed you and your friends my little fleet footed girl but this time I know who you are. Tell your little troupe I look forward to meeting them, soon' It disappeared through the window and the curtains billowed, she could have sworn that window was closed.

Liam pushed the door against her back and when he met the resistance of her body he called out 'Janet is there something up against the door' she hesitated for a second before pulling the door open and started pretending to look through the pile on the carpet 'It's just me I thought I saw something glinting in the carpet and thought it might be the back off an earring I had lost'

Liam bent down and wiped her face with his sleeve 'You must have been drooling when you were sleeping hen, and how did I not notice you had your hair coloured, I like it, very gothic' he said taking a handful of her hair at the side of her face and sliding it through his fingers. She stood up and looked in the mirror above her wall mounted electric fire and ran her own fingers through her hair. Well through the one inch wide streak of white that was now there.

She laughed it off by mumbling something about him never looking at her properly anymore and claimed a headache. She told him it would be better if he went home she wasn't feeling very well. In reality she was anxious to get in touch with the others as quickly as she could, but then the thought struck her that if that thing was still outside she could be sending Liam to his death.

'Here put this on' she said taking the crucifix from her neck and holding it out to him.

He burst out laughing 'I don't think so Jan it doesn't go with my tattoo' She looked at his tattoo and for the first time realised what it was, it was a Glasgow Rangers football crest with 'Aye Ready' below it. When she had first seen it she had smirked because she thought it was alluding to his sexual prowess.

'That would probably burn my neck if I put it on at the very least it would give me a bad rash' he said before adding 'Look you don't actually look very well why don't you go up to your bed Jan and I'll doss down here on your comfy sofa and that way if you need anything through the night I can get it for you'

Janet smiled sweetly and said ' No look I think I might have to vomit, my stomach is looping the loop and you're a nice guy but I don't think we're at the stage where I can be comfortable with you holding my hair back while I look down the toilet for Ralph'

It took him a second to get the joke he couldn't have been much of a *Billy Connolly* fan. He conceded defeat and slipped his shoes on and lifted his jacket from the chair he went to kiss her on the cheek and she flinched slightly. He stepped back and said 'what happened when I went upstairs for a hit and a miss Jan, when I went up you were snoozing and when I came back down you looked like you had seen a ghost. Oh for god's sake it's that stupid film that frightened you isn't it. I should have known when we were in *Blockbusters* you did say that you thought horror films were shite'

'No Liam it wisnae the film, actually it's a really bad menstrual cycle I am having in fact when I went to the toilet to change my *Tampax* the blood was coming out of me in clots just about'

That shifted him; he was out the door in three seconds flat. She giggled to herself that menstruation wisnae the best thing to talk about when a vampire was after you. Anyway, he wasn't as good looking as she thought he was in the club when she met him, he definitely wasn't as good looking as *he* thought he was, he was also a bigoted Ranger's supporter her dad would do her in if he seen her out with a stupid hun and worst of all what was this shite calling her Jan? She didn't call him Li did she?

She picked up the phone and dialled Maggie's number, no answer. Where could she be it was a Sunday night there's no way she would be out, maybe she would be in the bath. A vision presented itself to Janet. Maggie lying in a nice hot bath surrounded with bubbles and a face cloth over her face and just outside her bathroom window was that thing licking its manky chops. She let out a tiny squeal and tried dialling my number, but she was all fingers and thumbs. After a couple of tries she got through and it was Julie Anne my second wife of all of four years that answered the phone.

'Naw he's out at the pub with that bloody waster Stevie, and no I don't know which pub' was her reply to Janet's enquiry of whether I was in or not. Fortunately Janet did get a hold of Sonny on her first try and he managed to get Stevie on Stevie's brand new *Motorola* mobile phone. I was with Stevie, we were in *The Scotia bar* listening to a punter tell us about a Vampire scare there in the seventies apparently the place was still haunted by a former landlord who hung himself in the cellar around the same time.

We made a bee line for Maggie's house it wasn't that far away she was living at that time in a semi-detached in Kinning park. We took a taxi which couldn't have taken any more than fifteen minutes to get there. Janet and Sonny still managed to get there before us. They were getting no answer and Janet was becoming frantic, I must admit I had an ominous feeling in the pit of my stomach as well.

'That's the beauty of these things' Stevie said holding up his mobile phone if she had one of these we would know where she is.

'Aye as long as we were standing beside her, they things are shite, it's almost impossible to get through to you and then I canny hear a thing when you do answer' Sonny complained.

'You got me tonight but didn't you. I'm telling you within a couple of years you'se will all have one and what's more they are working on making the battery a bit smaller as well.' Stevie said.

'What are you a fuckin phone salesman, Maggie might be lying in there with her throat ripped out and all you can do is go on about your stupid phone' Janet said taking the Motorola from him and throwing it away. It broke in two when it bounced off Maggie's path.

'They're not very robust are they Stevie' Maggie asked as she got out of a taxi. 'This is a nice wee surprise to see all of you here, is it my birthday or something?' She was struggling with both hands full of Tesco bags. I took three bags from her as did Stevie. Janet announced to Maggie 'He's back Maggie look what he did to me' Holding the strand of white hair out for inspection.

Stevie just had to get his joke in 'That's a bit of a come down for him, is it no'? One of the lords of darkness coming back as a hairdresser' it was only him that laughed.

Janet busied herself making a pot of tea and putting out a plate of *Tunnock's Caramel Logs* the one's with all the coconut round them. Maggie used to work in the factory and still went along to the staff shop from time to time to fill her biscuit barrel up with seconds. I always thought the seconds she got were better than what they sold in the shops, you would get great big lumps of caramel in them or all caramel and no wafer, and they were superb. But that's not exactly what I was trying to tell you is it?

Maggie had an announcement of her own 'I knew he was back, he already spoke to me. I didn't believe it was him at first but now I know that it was, I'll tell you what happened first Janet and then you tell me what happened tonight okay?' Janet nodded her agreement she still looked pallid and scared. I looked from Janet to Maggie and wondered at their ability to keep functioning under these circumstances. The look on Sonny's face told me he was thinking the same thing. Stevie was too preoccupied with trying to put his phone back together to notice what anybody was doing, saying or thinking.

'It was last night, I was in the bath all bubbled up and feeling pleasantly drowsy' she said with a small smile on her lips. My whispering 'mmmm' didn't put her off her story but it did get me a disapproving glance, from Janet not Maggie strangely enough.

'I heard a fluttering at the bathroom window, which I ignored it thinking it was probably a Robin or a Sparrow trying to find a warm corner to build a nest. But it was insistent and it started to get a little bit louder and more frantic, it sounded as if whatever bird it was it was hurting itself. I stood up and put a towel round me intending to open the window, I had to because it's a frosted window in my bathroom and I couldn't see a thing through it. It's also high up, just as I stood on the toilet pan to open the window I felt a wee shiver run down my spine and saw what looked like the shape of a face in the top corner of the bathroom window. I hesitated and that was enough to cause that thing to get annoyed'

'Open the window Margaret, I command thee!' it said in a deep voice like some big Judge in the high court or something. For a start nobody has called me Margaret since my wee Granny Keenan died in 1976 and nobody has 'commanded' me to do anything ever in my life, so I wasn't gonnae start listening to commands now, do you know what I mean like' She paused in her story so that everyone could agree with her 'Aye' 'You're damn tooting' and 'I hope you telt the dickhead' were amongst the comments of approval she got.

'At this time I had no idea what or who it was in fact I wasn't even sure until you lot turned up tonight. I said to it 'why don't you fuck off away from my window before I throw a pot of boiling water over you ya stoat the ball. I don't know why I called him a stoat the ball because that's somebody that interferes with weans and I'm a far cry from being a wean' she looked quickly round the three boys and made us think twice before making any sarcastic remarks.

She continued 'I swear I heard this thing hiss and spit and as it left the window I thought I heard it say, *'this time I have the upper hand'* I shouted after it 'upper hand you bastard it's an upper cut you'll be getting if I have my way' she looked so angry all the rest of us could do was laugh.

'Who do you think you are Muhammad Ali' I asked. 'More like Jim watt' Maggie replied 'wee and Scottish but with a good bit of fight'

'So that was that' it was gone. I never got a wink of sleep all night and have been out of the house all day feart to come home. But eventually I thought no damn it, that's ma house and come what may I'm sleeping in my own bed' she said with determination.

'It's lucky you didnae open the windae, it would have been all over you in a shot, That's all these vampires need is for you to open the windae to them, it's like an invitation to them to do what they like to you. Just like it is when you let a man get his haun in your scants' Stevie suggested.

'What is wrong with you, you've no' long turned thirty and you still talk and snigger like a bloody twelve year old' Janet reprimanded him and backed it up with a sweet strike to the back of his head with her open palm.

'Hoy you, it's her that thinks she's Jim Watt no' you. That was bloody sore' Stevie said whilst he simultaneously rubbed his head and his knee which he had banged on the table trying to get away from Janet's slap.

'Stop being an arsehole and maybe she will stop slapping you' Sonny advised him.

'That's really not fair hitting him for being an arsehole Janet. That's like belting a dog for peeing against a lamppost' Stevie took a few seconds to grin, the others didn't.

'Hold on a minute it was badly put but the dim one in the corner does have a point. You're supposed to have to invite a vampire in before it can enter your house so how come it was lying behind you licking your face Janet?' I asked.

'Probably that moron you were seeing let it in before he went for a piss, thinking it was a pizza delivery or something' sonny suggested.

'It doesn't really matter now' Maggie said 'But it means you have to stay away from that house Janet, once it's invited in you canny un-invite it. A bit like the bold boy over there eh?' she added pointing at Stevie who was staring out of the window.

'Tam, Sonny come and look at this' Stevie said with an expression of alarm on his face.

He was pointing at a bush across the road from Maggie's house it was partly obscured by a bus stop so it was difficult to see what was happening to it. What I could see was a mist building up around about it and what looked like a hunched man appearing to walk through it. Straight at us.

'Is it him' Janet asked pressing against my back to get a better view.

'Naw it canny be he would have a big black cape on with a red lining. No' red chino's and a denim bomber jacket' Stevie offered us his sartorial opinion.

Whoever it was stopped thirty feet short of Maggie's window, in the middle of the road and pointed straight at us and laughed. 'Come on out to play children, you don't have your innocence to protect you this time' he said and held one hand out and beckoned us with his index finger which had a long curled black nail on it.

'Ok fuck face let's boogie' Sonny said and ran to Maggie's door. Stevie got there before him and said 'Let me take him Sonny. I've got a crucifix on and I stink of garlic, I smell like a French chef's arsehole' He was out through the door before any of us could stop him. He moved warily towards this guy, who , apart from the manky fingernail could be anybody standing at a bus stop waiting for a number nineteen into the town.

'Steven my little laggard. You were last out of the boxes the last time, is that why you are first this time? Have you been feeling guilty when you see Tam's scar. Have you been thirsting for another square go with me Stevie pal' the vampire if that's what it was had changed its voice from that of an English gentleman to one you would normally hear from a ned from the worst schemes in Glasgow.

'Cum oan then Stevie let's see wit you've goat big man. I'm not scared eh you by the way. Why wood ah be scared eh a jobby jabber, have you told all your buddies about you and wee touch your toes for Tony. Aye Maggie your ma's wee Italian stallion had a hard on for wee boys and some wee boys had a hard on for him Stevie boy didn't they' the thing shouted at Stevie as he circled it.

'Don't worry Stevie boy your secrets safe Tony is dead now I supped his essence and gave his body to my little soldiers' as it said this we saw four or five huge rats emerge from the sides of the bush and sit up their haunches and stare at us as they played with their whiskers.

'You're a lying bastart, I never let Tony touch me I didnae' Stevie screamed at it and ran towards it. It glided in a slow motion blur as it swooped at him with its claw like hand and immediately retreated holding something shiny aloft.

'I thoat so ya fud' it said brandishing Stevie's crucifix like a trophy 'you hif to believe in this shite for it tae work ya stupit fanny' it moved in a blur again towards him, but was stopped in its tracks by Maggie brandishing her own tiny cross. 'I believe' she said and grabbed its wrist just above its hand as it reached for Stevie's throat. She had the crucifix in the hand she grabbed it with. It shrieked as it flew away from them with smoke still rising from its injured wrist. The shape of cross was burned into it.

'Well well Maggie the maiden rides to the rescue' it said regaining its previous refined accent. 'Have you not told Tam that he is the one yet? The one you are holding out for. The one meant to deflower you in a field of golden barley drifting gently in the summer breeze. Have you told him that that's the vision in front of your eyes when you pleasure yourself' it said lasciviously licking its lips and revealing its curved and very pointed sharp teeth.

'I've told him thanks for killing you the last time you pathetic mongrel. But I'm telling him now, that this time it's me that gets to plunge a stake through your rotten smelly heart' she said It swatted the stick away with ease 'You really need to do better than that my little virgin tease.' It said as it glided out of her way and put its back to the bush and the rats got excited at their master coming within their reach. 'Are ye missing your ma hen' the monster said to Maggie 'She tasted like a rancid bottle of Buckie, but needs must eh?'

Maggie flew at it but tripped over two fat rats that ran under her feet as she approached within inches of their lord and master.

'Stevie ya fanny, I'll see you later ma man. Me and you are gonnae faw out big time, bring your wee fenian cross if you want tae, I can use it to tan your jaw before I rip your fuckin throat oot man' it said and disappeared into the mist surrounding the bush. Before it had completely disappeared I burst out laughing and shouted at it 'I've just realised, you've been biting the heads off of some Gorbals neds haven't you that's why you keep sounding like one. That must be a kick in the balls arsehole what with you being an educated man and all that' It hesitated and turned back towards me it's eyes glowed red and I heard it say inside my head 'You and I have unfinished business Thomas, should I tell them about your first wife and your experiments with tasting her blood. Go on Thomas dare me again' it was my turn to hesitate and say nothing, it slipped into the mist where it had come from.

'Get back in the house' Sonny said to all of us walking backwards towards the gate with his arms spread wide 'but don't turn your back, I don't think it's away yet'

No sooner had he said it than the thing burst from the bushes straight at Stevie and swiped its hand across his stomach and was away before any of us could react. As Stevie stood watching the blood ooze through his Canary yellow *Lyle and Scott* pullover and run through his fingers, all we could hear was 'ha ha ya fanny I told you I was gonnae do you, wan nothing to me ya fud'

Stevie sank to his knees and said 'That wee fuckin ned has ripped me Tam' and then collapsed onto his face in the street.

It took the ambulance fifteen minutes to get there and another ten to get him to the Southern General hospital, Maggie and Janet went in the ambulance with him. Sonny and I followed sedately with a taxi driver who had no sense of urgency despite being told we were anxious about our friend that had been stabbed. If anything it made him drive slower.

When we eventually got to the hospital half an hour after the ambulance had arrived Sonny said to the driver as we climbed out of the back of his cab 'Are you expecting a tip' the driver looked at him warily and nodded yes 'Okay then don't be a prick all your life, and here's your fare' Sonny handed him one pound fifty.

'The fare was two quid, I will be getting the polis to you' the taxi driver threatened.

'The only thing you will be getting is the toe of my size nines up your hole pal' I said and walked towards the cab, the driver got the message and did a quick spin before shooting away.

'Size nine's? That's a bit wee Tam I take a size 12, and you know what they say about men with big feet don't you' Sonny smiled.

'Aye they are born to be clowns, are you turning into Stevie as some sort of sympathy act ya fanny' I asked him, he grinned as we hustled into the accident and emergency department.

Janet and Maggie were sitting in a busy waiting room holding hands. Maggie looked relieved when she saw us come in and I could see why. There was a junkie sitting straight across from them and he had clearly been harassing them, presumably for money. This we could do without tonight.

'On your way pal' Sonny said to him and kicked the leg of the chair the junkie was sitting on.

'It's no' your hospital big man I could get you done for assault, gies a fiver and I will make like a gun and shoot' the junkie said much to his own amusement. This is why I hate Glasgow hospitals they are full of arseholes like him, you can't get moving for them. But his whiny wee Ned voice was reminding me of earlier and getting on my nerves. I hooked my foot under the front of his chair and flipped him backwards and he tumbled his wilkies off the chair and banged his head against the bottom of the vending machine. Somebody must have jammed some change in the slot because as soon as his head hit the machine two fifty pence coins and a ten pence piece fell to the floor beside him. He looked at them and scooped them up in a single swipe 'Result, cheers big man' he said and strolled away like he had just won a million on black at the casino.

We sat down Maggie was the first to speak 'They have taken him into theatre it's a deep cut, the doctor asked if he had been fighting a bear, and no he didn't mean a Rangers supporter' she smiled but it didn't reach her eyes.

Janet added her tuppence worth 'He did say that Stevie would be fine though didn't he Maggie? I heard him say that'

'He said that Stevie was a young man and fit and healthy and he should do okay' Maggie responded with little enthusiasm or belief.

'Fit and healthy my arse' I said 'they obviously haven't tested him for drugs for a while' I wasn't really angry at Stevie, but the man, the thing, I was angry at wasn't here. We spent a long four hours waiting for Stevie to emerge from under the knife. He eventually did and the prognosis was good. No internal organs had been damaged; the wound was ragged and required multiple stitches but would heal albeit with a nasty scar.

Janet volunteered to stay with Stevie until he could look after himself; she was concerned with the ease at which our adversary had snatched the crucifix from his neck. It appeared to be true that the cross without the belief was a useless ornament. She asked one of the nurses if she could check the hospital kitchen for any spare garlic. The nurse looked at her as if she wanted to admit her for psychiatric tests. Janet tried to make out that it was a homeopathic way to ward off infection and that the Chinese use it in hospitals. The nurse wasn't convinced, by her assurances but seemed more convinced of her insanity.

Janet made us wait until she nipped down to Govan cross and bought all the garlic she could find. The nurses complained bitterly at the smell, but when Janet declared herself to be Stevie's wife and soul mate, an assertion that was supported by all of us they let her do her stuff, but still continued to whisper to each other and point at her, as anyone would have.

Sonny, Maggie and I shared a taxi back to Maggie's house with the intention of settling in and making plans to go after the vampire. We decided against it when we arrived at her house and it was overrun with rats, not pet rats either, dirty smelly sewer rats. The stench was appalling as soon as the taxi door opened the driver even remarked that someone had drain problems and they were going to be spending a fortune to put it right.

Maggie was determined to clear them from her house and picked up a garden rake from the garden. Sonny and I had to virtually drag her away kicking and screaming. We had no choice we had to there was literally thousands upon thousands of rats. We could see from outside as they climbed curtains and ran across window ledges inside all of the rooms. There was even twenty or more coming out of the chimney pots onto the roof.

'Come on we can go to mine' I said.

'No my flat's nearer and Sylvia won't mind' Sonny said.

'I want to tell the authorities' Maggie said.

'What authorities Maggie, Polis, fire brigade or ambulance service take your pick, which one of them will listen to a tale about a vampire that talks like a ned one minute and john Major the next' I asked.

'Let's go to the polis, we don't need to tell them he is a vampire. We can just tell them we think somebody is targeting vulnerable people in the Gorbals' she suggested.

'It would never work Maggie; they would pap us in the cells and call for the men with white coats' I said.

'I know a polis that might listen' Sonny said.

'Well let's go see him Sonny, there's no time like the present' Maggie insisted.

'It's a her actually' Sonny said.

As we turned to leave we heard a phone ring and quickly realised it was Stevie's mobile contraption. It was lying at Sonny's feet; he bent down and picked it up. It couldn't be working it was in bits with wires hanging out of the side. But it kept on ringing; he held it up to his ear and then snatched it away quickly. He smiled and said 'There was a lot of static but the man wants us to know that he hopes we have a nice day because after all it will be our last'

....

'I have had a think about what you told me and I have found a couple of odd things that I want one of you to explain' Detective Sergeant Christina Newton said looking directly at me.

'We can try but you are unlikely to believe us' I replied for all of us. We had played down the vampire element and told this very understanding police woman about how we suspected there might be a killer targeting people in the Gorbals.

She smiled pleasantly at me and said 'you would be surprised at what I would believe, why haven't any of you said that you think there is a vampire in the Gorbals killing children?'

We all looked at each other and then looked at her sceptically, 'We get all kinds of nutcase's in here' she said and smiled 'Present company excluded at the moment, but tell me everything and I can make up my mind whether you deluded crackpots or concerned citizens'

Maggie looked at me 'What have we got to lose Tam, all she can do is laugh at us and pap us out' But it wasn't as simple as that, to tell her the whole story we would need to include what happened in the Southern Necropolis on Hogmanay in 1974. Depending on how you looked at that night, we were a band of heroic teenagers who saved the Gorbals from a blood sucking monster. Or a bunch of teenage Ned's who killed a defenceless old man and stuffed him into an old crypt.

I compromised I would tell her everything that was happening now and be vague about our involvement in 1974. She listened carefully to everything we told her and asked us to hang about for half an hour so she could think it through. She got us some coffee's which judging by the taste of it was for prisoner's consumption only.

She came back into the interview room with two bulging files sealed with string she threw them on the table which released a mini cloud of dust. 'In here are files from 1953/54 and 1973/74 and this one is from the last six months' she said placing another thinner file on the table. 'We do get deranged old women in here saying they have seen everything from Jesus Christ on a bus to Frankenstein's monster behind the co-op. And in all of those files you will find some of them and beside them you will find statements from doctors, lawyers, and in one case in 1954 a sitting Sherriff. None of these are active files they are all dormant there isn't a single Strathclyde police officer out there hunting vampires, strangely enough'

'So will you be the first then? Sonny asked her. It was Sonny who had brought us to see Christina she was a former school friend of his wife and they had discussed Sonny's 'hobby' of researching stories of the paranormal in and around Glasgow. Sonny had told his wife nothing of 1974 and very little of what was happening now. Nor had I told my wife, it's a sort of difficult subject to bring up. 'Listen sweetheart watching that film has just reminded me, back in 1974 me and some of my wee pals stabbed a vampire through the heart with a sharpened baseball bat and disposed of his body'

Christina pondered for a second and said 'I can't do anything official but I am going to have an unofficial gander round the Gorbals. Maybe talk to some of the dealers and junkies; they know everything that's going on. They are watching out for us so much that they see everything else as well. If you want to know who's up to what in an area any area ask the junkies and dealers'

'So that's it' Maggie asked with thinly veiled disgust. Christina didn't take the bait she just nodded and gave a slight shrug of her shoulders 'at the moment Maggie, aye that's all I can do'

A week passed without incident, without any vampire related incident coming to our attention I mean. Quite a bit had happened in our lives; Stevie had got out of hospital and moved in with Sonny and his wife Sylvia. He was getting about not so bad but had indulged himself with a silver tipped Cherry wood walking stick like some bloody squire or something. He would tap it on Sonny's coffee table when he needed a beer brought through from the fridge. It was a safe bet to assume that at some point in the next few weeks that walking stick and Stevie's arse were going to become intimate.

To make it more awkward Sonny had decided he couldn't keep the truth from Sylvia any longer so had told her everything. She couldn't or wouldn't believe him and her behaviour had become very erratic. She was on the phone every day to her friend Christina the detective sergeant. Begging to be told that Sonny was wrong there were no such things as vampires. Christina humoured her as much as she could but refused to say Sonny was wrong in all of his assumptions.

This inspired me to tell my wife some of the story as well. Not everything, I had been married to Julie Anne for less than four years. We had been put together as a blind date by mutual friends, and it's probably true to say that there was a lack of a real spark between us. However we got on well enough and as time passed we gradually moved in together and that led to a simple wedding ceremony at Martha street registry office.

I think it probably took us a maximum of two years for both of us to realise that we had drifted into a marriage of convenience. We had both been on the rebound from long term relationships and had probably opted for the comfort of a partner without the volatility that passion brings. We had been drifting along the last couple of years just because separation would be more of a pain than it was worth. Strangely the current situation had interested Julie Anne more than anything we had done since we got married. She was highly intrigued, demanded to know more and even begged to be included in any further shenanigans as she put it. I promised to try and include her but was reluctant to lay bare my soul and my past to her. For one thing it was very painful what we did in 74 still haunts me and for another thing Julie Anne in all reality was almost a stranger to me.

I promised to try and include her where I could and inadvertently did so when the whole thing came to a head and a deadly conclusion just eight days after it put Stevie in hospital. The night before Christina called Maggie and advised her that she had some vital information and a very strong lead. She asked Maggie to make sure that everyone came to Sonny's house that evening.

I arrived with Maggie and Julie Anne at Sonny's West end flat it was in an old sandstone tenement building on Byres road. Maggie had met up with Julie Anne and me at four o'clock that afternoon just to catch up. There was a frisson of electricity between the two of them. I suspect they both had suspicions about my relationship with the other. Maggie got over it first. She was concerned more about Christina, whom she had been keeping in daily contact with until three nights previous. Then Christina stopped answering both of her phones, her house phone and her mobile phone. Although she did get Christina's mother during one attempt to speak to her, her mother hadn't heard from her for three days and was concerned.

Maggie tried her at work but was told she had taken a leave of absence. We wondered whether perhaps she had escalated the investigation and was working undercover. This now seemed likely since she wanted to meet us this evening.

Sylvia let us in, I have never see a woman look as anxious as she did that night, she seemed petrified by something. I tried to ask her when I went to help her with the teas and coffee but she refused to be drawn into any kind of conversation. I couldn't help but be affected by her extreme nervousness everyone there was getting very jumpy by the time Christina showed up.

She didn't arrive until almost ten o'clock which was a bit rude really and then she went all weird, Janet opened the door to her when she knocked and she refused to come in until Sylvia came out and insisted 'Please come in you and yours are welcome in my house' Sylvia said all very formally. The hairs on the back of my neck were beginning to stand up and Maggie also looked wired. Something was wrong with Christina, the split second I noticed that was enough time for 'it' to appear from behind Sylvia coming from the direction of the kitchen. It grabbed Julie Anne and dragged her unceremoniously into a corner of the living room. It stood poised behind her and gently eased her long black hair away from the side of her throat and presented its teeth to us.

I heard a hissing sound behind me and saw Christina lunge at Sylvia and pull her into the opposite corner. 'It' spoke to me 'Choose one Tam the Sham'.

'Choose one what' I asked.

'One to live one to die, your choice, choose'

Julia Anne's eyes beseeched me, Sylvia was behind me, I couldn't see her eyes but I could see Sonny's they were flat and lifeless and told me nothing.

'I won't choose, I can't choose. I will give you a choice, set them free and you and I can settle this between us. We can close the doors just you and I nobody else need be involved'

'Is it a square go you want then' It screeched in its ned voice and turned punched a hole right through the brick wall into the living room, then swivelled back and with one downward sweep of its hand smashed Sylvia's lovely wood effect worktop into pieces 'Are you sure?' it asked.

It was the wrong time for humour I know but I responded 'come ahead big man I'm gonny do you' in *my* best Ned voice. This seemed to infuriate it and it lifted Julie Anne by the throat and stretched its arms until she was at least two feet above his head and her feet were dangling by his knees. Janet and Maggie had been conspiring behind my back as I engaged 'it' in conversation. They chose this moment to go on the attack. Janet leapt at the vampire crucifix in her outstretched hand and she scored a direct hit on his left cheek. The crucifix welded itself to his cheek he had nowhere to run and nowhere to hide. Sonny surged forward and grabbed a shard of the broken worktop, lifted it and stabbed it into the creature's heart. But not before it had plunged its teeth into Julie Anne's neck then broke her back over its knee and tossed her aside like a bundle of dirty washing.

On the other side of the room Christina hissed and tried to sink her teeth into Sylvia's neck but before she could break the skin Maggie pulled her head back by the hair and pressed her own crucifix into Christina's forehead. As her skin sizzled and burned Stevie took one step forward and thrust his walking stick so hard through Christina on an upward trajectory that she was lifted and hung on the wall like a pinned moth.

Sylvia fainted and Sonny ran to her side, I turned back towards the vampire but it was gone. The kitchen window was gently banging against the nearest cabinet and the curtains fluttered in the breeze.

Chapter five; Stevie P's flat Jan 6th 2015

We were all remembering what happened to Christina Newton and Julie Anne in 1994 more so we were remembering the aftermath.

Within minutes of the vampires doing his latest disappearing act the walking stick pinning Christina to the wall broke free and she slid to the floor. Her appearance started to change the pallor left her complexion and the black rings around her eyes faded. What was more amazing was the walking stick being ejected from her body and the hole it had made healing up. She almost looked as if she had fallen asleep on the floor. Her eyes flickered open but only for the briefest second, long enough for her to look at Stevie and mouth 'thank you' before they closed and she was still.

The process was repeated with Julie Anne, she lay dead at Christina's feet her throat gaping and blood spilled down her dress. What we saw next will haunt me forever; it was like slow motion time lapse photography in reverse. The blood formed little globules which ran back up her dress and into her body, the gash that the vampire had torn in her throat slowly healed itself and calm reappeared on Julie Anne's features, she too looked asleep.

'That means he's dead' Stevie said.

'She's dead' I corrected him.

'Naw no' Julie Anne, him, the vampire. These two healing like that means he's dead. I saw it in a film' he said with an air of certainty.

'This isn't a fuckin film moron' I said with more cruelty than I intended, I was angry and he was an easy target.

Stevie never did mind playing the target for any of us 'I know it's no' a film Tam, I was just saying'

Neither Sonny nor his wife Sylvia had seen any of this. The moment the vampire vanished Sylvia had become hysterical, and had remained hysterical since. Sonny walked her along their hall to a bedroom and tried to calm her down. We could still hear her wailing until the very second Christina mouthed thank you and then she stopped. All at once, completely.

In the silence I could feel a scream starting in my own throat, I was staring at my wife of four years and she was dead. I killed her. I murdered her by bringing her here, I knew the risks and she didn't. I killed her.

Maggie as usual brought us all back to the moment in her no nonsense reality mode.

'We need to tidy this up' she said spreading her hands wide.

I got angry at her, 'This isn't red wine spilled on the fuckin carpet Maggie. That's my wife lying there' Dead. In case you haven't noticed' I aid quietly it might have been better for me had I shouted.

'I know who it is Tam, I also know that over there is a police detective sergeant and that both women look asleep and they don't have a mark on them' she looked at me as if she wanted me to object to her analysis, I said nothing.

'Unless we all want to go to jail, we need to think our way out of this' she said.

'What if he's not dead' Janet asked, she had barely moved since she had thrust her crucifix against Christina's forehead.

'He is' came a chorused reply from Maggie, Stevie, Me and Sylvia who had appeared from nowhere. She looked glassy eyed, almost as if she was stoned. Maybe she was, maybe Sonny had slipped her a Mickey Finn in the bedroom.

'He is at rest he is sleeping the sleep of the un-dead' Sylvia said in a monotone.

We stared at her waiting for more nothing came. 'Well that's awfully nice for him but what are we going to do' Maggie said returning full blown to her organiser persona.

'I am taking Julie Anne home; I will dress her in her nightgown and put her to bed. I will call an ambulance and never admit being anywhere near here or any of you ever. If they don't believe me they don't believe me. It is what it is' I said quietly, I knew in my heart that Julie Anne's death was my fault and I would take whatever punishment came my way.

'Good Tam, that's good. It's right that you should look after Julie Anne' Maggie said and added. 'Sonny I need you to help me with Christina. We need to take her somewhere she will be found quickly'

Sonny looked over at Maggie and said 'I can't I need to look after Sylvia'

'Sylvia's alive she can look after herself, I need your help Sonny. Tam is taking his wife home and Stevie is just out of hospital, I need you Sonny' Maggie said like a football coach getting a player to get with the programme.

'Maggie, Sylvia needs me more' he said and guided Sylvia out of the kitchen back towards the bedroom. She moved like a robot with low batteries, she was clearly in deep shock.

'I will help you Maggie, I'm not that bad' Stevie said as he stood up with a grunt.

'Aye great idea Stevie why don't you burst your stitches and bleed all over her' Janet said 'I'll help you Maggie, where should we take her. I've got my wee mint parked outside'

Janet's wee mint was her 1982 *Volkswagen Polo* which was more temperamental than a ballerina on steroids. Maggie could see that Stevie was incapable, Sonny was unwilling and that I had my own hands full. She nodded at Janet and glared in Sonny's direction. There were two walls between them but I had a feeling he could feel that glare on his back.

I found out later that Maggie and Janet had left Christina in a dark bus stop near Maxwell Park and telephoned an ambulance claiming they saw a drunken woman lying down apparently asleep in a bus stop. They waited fifteen minutes for the ambulance to arrive and then went back to Janet's house where they had left Stevie. Maggie's house was still being fumigated to rid it of rats. The story of her infestation had cause a fuss for a day or two after it was reported in the *Evening Times* as '*Rat lady flees infestation*' the more moronic Glaswegians thought she was infested with fleas, and were even more horrified when they saw the photographs of a few hundred dead rats. They would have been even worse if they had seen the thousands of live ones.

I treated Julie Anne with perfect respect and did what I could to preserve her dignity. The police interviewed me for fourteen hours straight. Thirty two year old women don't just lie down and die. The police were convinced it was a drug related death, when they had first arrived at my house a detective had actually lifted her arm looking for needle tracks until I pushed him away and tried to punch him. I told them nothing. My story was that I sat and watched a video on my own. Julie Anne came home early from work not feeling great; she decided to have a bath and an early night. When I had decided it was my bed time I discovered her lifeless body and phoned an ambulance.

One detective grilled me endlessly as to why I was showing so little emotion. I shrugged my shoulders and told him it's the way I am. The truth was I wouldn't cheapen Julie Anne's memory by trying to put an act on for the police. He couldn't see inside me at the guilt that was spreading like a cancer, I could feel it. They eventually let me go and when the post mortem results the following week showed no drugs and no injuries the coroner had no choice but to record the death as *Sudden Adult Death Syndrome*. I had never heard of it but apparently it was similar to cot death in babies but not as frequent.

The police came back with a vengeance two weeks later, a colleague had found Christina Newton's notebook and discovered that I had met her a week before her death. Her death had also been put down to *Adult Sudden death syndrome*. The detectives at Orkney street police station did not like coincidences very much at the best of times. But two women dying inexplicable deaths on the same night in Glasgow and me knowing both of them was way beyond coincidence in their humble opinion. My arse was toast as they say.

I spent 72 hours in police custody telling re-telling and telling again the story of that night. I added nothing I took nothing away, I was rigid. They played good cop bad cop, they woke me up at three in the morning, they let me go eight hours without even a cup of tea or a slice of bread. They put a supposed nutcase in beside me who tried to get me to open up. They put a psycho in beside me who told me that the police had offered to let him walk if he gave me a wee kicking. I refused to have a lawyer present; I insisted I had done nothing wrong. There was a relatively young female detective constable, this was her first case. She looked as if she was welling up most of the time but kept her composure reasonably well. Christina Newton had been her mentor.

This DC Simpson, Helen Simpson, told me she that if I walked out with no charges against me she would spend the rest of her life shadowing me until she could put me away where I belonged. I told her 'Okay, that's fair enough' that got me my one and only slap from a police officer during those 72 hours. The other officer in the interview room shook his head at Helen as he said to me 'I didn't quite see what happened their Mr Mundell, do you wish me to get a complaint form from the front desk sir'

'Naw' I said and some of the guilt I was feeling must have shown in my eyes because Helen Simpson saw it and gasped 'you do know something' I slowly shook my head. What I knew would never be told to her or anyone else outside my circle of vampire hunters. We had involved other people and look what happened it wouldn't be happening again.

Against their better judgement they released me, they had also quizzed the others who had been present at the meeting with Christina Newton and coincidentally were friends of mine, they had all given each other cast iron alibi's and the police eventually had to drop it, but they pursued us relentlessly. I think we must have been on a most wanted list. Over the next six months we had twenty two speeding tickets between us. Two of us had been done for littering and Stevie the half-wit was done for possession of a class A drug. Luckily for him it was considered too small a quantity to be anything other than personal use.

Eventually it went away, it stopped being a story in the newspaper and we stopped being targeted by the Glasgow police. The guilt never went away it still hasn't time has given me the perspective to say that Julie Anne was an adult who insisted on being involved. But time hasn't given me the perspective to believe that shit and forgive myself.

'So here we go again troops' Stevie said bringing me out of my reverie.

'Indeed we do' Maggie agreed.

I rubbed my face with both hands and said 'I'm too fuckin old for this shite guys. I'm too fucking old. I vote we find some young pups tell them the score and ruin their fuckin lives the way ours have been ruined' I honestly believe that idea was given momentary consideration that's how weary we were of this.

'Sonny, you're *Google Beard* what have you got for us?' Janet asked. Sonny had been given the task of researching whatever he could find about our adversary. He had been nicknamed *Google Beard* because he had an extremely irritating habit of launching into Google the minute anybody asked a question. You couldn't say 'What was the name of that Humphrey Bogart film he was in with Lauren Bacall before he was pounding away on his laptop or tablet to come up with the answer, he refused to stop it even when we told him he was killing every decent conversation we ever had. The beard part was because he had suddenly grown an Osama Bin laden style beard from nowhere. I must confess I also toyed with a goatee for a while at the end of 2014 when it seemed that everybody had facial hair of some sort. But Sonny grew a world class beard in four months and like anything else he treated criticism of it as water of a ducks back or in his case *Guinness* off a weirdo's beard. Sonny smiled at the *Google Beard* dig; secretly I think he liked it. 'I think I know who this guy is' he announced in his deadpan manner, and by my reckoning he is just over 142 years old on his last birthday which was December the 25th'

I laughed and said 'that's it Sonny has lost the plot, He thinks this guy is Santa fuckin clause'

The others didn't laugh they had more respect for Sonny's normally super accurate information than I had.

Sonny dismissed my stupidity with a withering glance in my direction our enemy's name is 'Pere noel' he said.

'Fuck off that's French for Father Christmas ya fanny' I yelled at him.

'I know I'm only winding you up ya dobber, the vampires name is Roderick Fitzgerald Murray' he said with a flourish and handed us all a binder with ten pages in it. He really could be an arsehole at times, all he had to do was tell us the story but he had to make a power point presentation meal of it. I wish I had never encouraged him to buy a fuckin PC.

What his ten pages boiled down to was that Roddy Murray (let's call him that just for convenience) had been born in the slums of Govan in 1872. But had bettered himself by learning to read and write, this learning was done at the feet of an old man called Cosmin Petrescu a Romanian who had come to Scotland as a prisoner after the

Crimean war. Young Roddy was a go getter and once he learned to read and write he begged stole and borrowed to become a solicitor which he did by the age of twenty nine.

His teacher, old Cosmin was dead by then but it appears as stranger came looking for old Cosmin one dark and miserable night and was pointed in the direction of his star pupil and rising star in legal circles, our very own Roddy Murray. This stranger like Cosmin hailed from the mountains of Romania and a very strange bird indeed was our stranger. His name was Alexendru Ghica. Let's call him Alex the Geek; Alex took the entire second floor of the Glasgow Central Hotel between the years 1901 to 1907. The hotel was being extensively renovated through those years so we can only imagine how much gold he had to part with to secure such a long tenancy.

Alex the Geek was an elusive figure he did however appear in the *Glasgow Evening News* on more than one occasion and was harangued by that newspaper for bringing shame on the name of the Central Hotel by holding debauched gatherings which were considered by the editor to be re-enactments of Sodom and Gomorrah. He also ran a few 'ripper' headlines when prostitutes were turning up with their throats savaged in the vicinity of Argyle Street. Alex took exception to this and used his by now faithful employee Roddy Murray to legally advise the said editor that he should desist from blackening Alex's name or face a duel.

As the newspapers were still reporting on what has been considered Scotland's last duel in 1899 between two Glasgow university students, a young Scottish student and a hot headed Italian boy. The idea of a possible duel between a newspaper editor and a visiting Nobleman, who by this time was being hailed as a Romanian prince, was causing considerable excitement amongst the gentry. Quite what a Romanian prince was doing in Argyle street remains a mystery. I could ask Sonny but don't think I will.

Like most disputes between big knobs in that era, this dragged on for a couple of years until the editor showed his mettle and challenged the prince to a square go on Glasgow Green. What he actually did was send his mate round with an invitation to duel. The prince agreed as long as the square go was at night. The editor said piss off; duels are always fought at dawn. You understand I'm paraphrasing here don't you. The upshot was that they couldn't agree a time and the whole situation slipped away when the prince buggered off back to Romania in 1907. But now we come to the interesting part, interesting for me at any rate. Before Alex the geek showed his face our Roddy Murray was a strapping young man of around thirty years old. Who had made an excellent start in carving out a fine reputation for himself in legal circles, and was almost a permanent fixture in both the Sherriff courts and the High courts. By 1902 one year after being employed by Alex the geek our Roddy was never seen in any court at all, he was only ever seen tagging along behind the geeks party-loving entourage when they were hitting the big lights of Glasgow city centre merrily debauching as they went along.

Roddy Fitzgerald Murray was hanged by the neck until he was dead in 1910. His crime according to the Glasgow Herald had been infanticide. He had been found in a back alley off the Gallowgate 'devouring a three week old baby'. A newspaper report of his hanging claims that a member of the crowd must have thrown a lighted torch as Mr Murrays clothes and skin were seen to *'flame and smoulder'* the hanging took place eight minutes after dawn on December the 25th.

The last page of Sonny's extensive report showed an article from The Daily Record dated December 26th 2014. It told the story of a hanging the previous day of one Roderick Fitzgerald Murray. The same Roderick Fitzgerald Murray who had been hanged until he was dead back in 1910. The article explained how it was believed that cohorts of Mr Murray had secreted his body away from the site and revived him in some way through medical prowess or some say witchcraft. His association with Alexendru Ghica was raised and aspersions cast on the Romany people as being complicit in raising him from the dead. This time he was hung with a stake through his heart and buried in an unrevealed grave at midnight.

'So who is it we are after, Alex or Roddy' Stevie asked and Janet nodded her agreement with the question.

'It's Roderick' Maggie answered, and we now know that banging a stake through his heart doesn't kill him permanently, it seems to make him lie dormant for twenty years or thereabouts but it doesn't kill him'

'So what does' I asked 'A silver bullet?'

'That's for a werewolf' Janet advised me.

'I read a book' Stevie started to say, to a spontaneous round of applause.

'Aye okay very funny, I read a book once, I think it was by Stephen King, and in it you had to cut off a vampires head and limbs and stuff the orifices with garlic to truly kill a vampire' he said.

'Are you sure that wasn't a book by Gordon Ramsay and it was a chicken and no' a vampire' I asked.

'Ha ha' was Stevie's sarcastic response.

We all looked at Sonny if anybody knew the answer it would be him. He shrugged his shoulders 'I think Stevie is probably right, quite a few novels suggest dismemberment and decapitation with the resultant cavities being filled with Garlic as the preferred disposal method,'

'Only you could make that sound like an instruction book from Ikea' I said, he rightly ignored me and continued.

'Unfortunately there aren't any training manuals for vampire hunters except novels. The existence of mythical creatures that suck the blood of animals and humans has been a subject of literature since man devised the written word. There are actually cave paintings in South America denoting hunters drinking the blood of their prey. Some tribes in both South America and Africa are said to still indulge in this practice. The tales of the eastern European vampires probably began with Vlad the Impaler. He was a kind of emperor back in the fifteenth century, by all accounts he was bit of an all-round bad bastard' Sonny paused to take another sheet of paper from his extensive file.

'There's a load of stuff on *Wikipedia* about him if your interested stuff like this' and he read us a passage 'He roasted children, whom he fed to their mothers. And he cut off the breasts of women, and forced their husbands to eat them. After that, he had them all impaled' so like I said a bit of a nutter. But that doesn't explain the un-dead angle or living forever. Bram Stoker sort of started that with his book about Dracula, the link there is that part of Vlad's family was called Dracula, so that's why people link them together.

Another idea of where the eternal life connection was made was about "Blood Countess" Elizabeth Báthory. She was an Hungarian countess who killed hundreds maybe thousands of young lassies, there were various rumours that she drank their blood or bathed in it to ensure eternal youth'

'Is this getting us anywhere Sonny?' I asked, I suppose it was interesting but I was more concerned with doing this guy in this time and I wasn't sure how going onto *Wikipedia* and reading about some tart with a blood fetish was going to help us do that.

'Failing to prepare means preparing to fail' Sonny replied pompously.

'I don't care what anybody says Sonny, sometimes you can be a complete fanny' I told him. His facial expression told me he agreed but didn't care.

Maggie then decided our next moves, as she always does. 'Sonny can you keep at it, we need to know as much as we can if we are going to end this for good' Sonny couldn't resist a little 'Fuck you' glance at me, as if he was the teacher's pet all of a sudden, fanny that he indubitably is.

Maggie kept talking 'Stevie get back in touch with Sinead and see if she has got any more news about the homeless people going missing, that Hamish Allan Centre is just along from the Gorbals that must mean something. Janet you go and see Agnes Lawrence's parents and see what they have to say. Tam' she hesitated probably unsure of what I had to offer other than sarcasm and profanity. 'Tam can you try and find out more about Roderick Murray. One thing I have read about vampires is that they will always try to sleep in the earth they were originally buried in. So maybe finding out where he was buried would help us track him down'

I wasn't sure why I was being given this task rather than Sonny. I didn't have his ability or patience to wade through the mountains of shit on the internet or in library's to find the occasional nugget. I used to do it but that was a while back. I asked 'Would that not be better for Sonny to do, you know how much I hate sitting at a screen for any longer than I need to.

Maggie smiled at me 'Sonny will do the real work, I wanted you to prowl round all the graveyards in Glasgow and see if you could find his grave or anything else that struck you as odd. Since you are the big shot writer with more spare time than *Harry Hills'* barber I thought you would have a better chance than any of us doing it'

She had me there; I did have more than ample free time. She was being slightly tongue in cheek about big shot writer; I had done a serious of novels in the late eighties which proved quite lucrative, particularly when a mini-series had been made from them. It hadn't made me super rich but I was in a position where I probably wouldn't have to take a real job for the rest of my life. I didn't really consider myself a writer anymore, not that I ever really had. I hadn't written anything of note since 1990 and didn't expect to anytime soon.

Thanks to *'Dave'* and the rest of the repeat channels on *Sky television* I still received quite sweet royalty payments on a fairly regular basis. But my writing days were over; I think probably that was another symptom of what we had gone through in 1994. Up to that point I had still been trying with little success to continue writing, but ever since then I haven't ever put pen to paper or nowadays fingertips to keyboard.

I nodded at her and agreed and asked Sonny to pass on any leads wherever he could and I would feed-back anything I learned to him. Maggie disagreed and asked everybody to report back to her and she would co-ordinate so that we weren't duplicating our efforts.

There is a determination about Maggie that gave her an inner beauty, I watched her put her hand on Janet's shoulder then plant a kiss on sonny's cheek. An arm round Stevie's waist, she was a general reassuring her troops before battle. A football captain inspiring from the middle of the huddle. She had been waiting for this moment, this was the real reason she wasn't married with children. This was her moment this was her time.

I was abruptly forced out of my reflection by my mobile going off, it loudly played *'You're the one that I want'* from *Grease.* June had developed a wicked little habit of changing my ring tones every time I left my phone in her presence. She assigned individual songs to my contact list. For example Steve had variously been *'Rhinestone Cowboy'* and *'The oldest swinger in town'* she had shown a barely concealed jealous streak by tagging Maggie with *'Jolene'* on more than one occasion.

'It's June' I needlessly announced. I turned away intending to take the call out in the hall if necessary but she didn't say a word she only screamed. And then dropped the phone and screamed again but from further away.

Chapter six Tam's ma's house 27th December 1974

'How can he be at the windae on the fifteenth floor that's mental? Do you mean he was out on the veranda' Stevie asked.

Janet found her voice 'He was outside my windae Stevie. I swear on the Holy Bible, he was crawling up the wall, he crawled up to the top of the window and he asked me to let him in. I said no, you're a ghost I'm no' letting you in. He spat the dummy out'

'How come?' I asked.

'He started banging his fists on the wall beside the window, it didnae make any noise but, so that just convinced me he was a ghost. Then he started greeting and begging me telling me how cauld he was and all that. He must have been fair freezing right enough his face was all blue.' She said starting in some way to enjoy the telling of the tale if not the tale itself.

'is he no' blue because he's dead' I asked as gently as a fourteen year old boy was capable of asking.

'Aye probably but it was freezing as well' she answered 'and the begging went on for another couple of minutes. I couldn'y stand it much longer and was just about to let him in, cause after all he is my wee brother. But I heard my ma in the hall coming towards my room. She could have been going to the toilet I suppose because that's past my room. But she wisnae she came into the room just as I was shutting the curtains, and she began talking to me so she couldn'y have seen Tommy'

'Aye you do right to shut the curtains hen, these bloody flats were put up in such a fuckin hurry they aren't even wind proof you could fly a fuckin kite in that hall some nights. Have you heard any news about Tommy yet hen?' she said.

'What could I do, I couldn'y say aye he's outside my window walking up a wall. Could i? I just said no ma, and she went back ben the living room. *the Onedin line'* was coming on she wouldn't want to miss that' Janet paused for breath.

'It's just as well you didnae let him in' Maggie told her quietly.

'How?' Janet asked just as quietly.

'Because he's a vampire now' Maggie replied with genuine regret on her face. 'I read all about them in my ma's journals, that's how they get in your house, they need to ask. If you had let him in you would all have been vampires by the morning'

'Aye I read that in a comic as well' Stevie agreed.

'I never seen that in the *Beano*' I said in my normal irritating way of trying to lighten the mood.

'No the *Beano* ya mongo. *Tales from the crypt* one of Sanny's American Comics' he replied missing the joke altogether. Sanny is Stevie's older brother he's twenty nine and still reads comics. He grew up in the sixties so he was probably still on an acid trip or something.

'We need to kill him' Sonny said softly. Janet sobbed 'We canny he's my wee brother, my ma would kill me if I killed him'

Maggie took control 'Tommy's already deid Janet, the thing that was at your windae isnae Tommy. It's a monster if we don't do something then it will get in somewhere and the Gorbals will be hoaching with vampires. We have to find it and kill it tonight or tomorrow we need to' Janet said nothing; she just continued to sob and managed a nod.

Stevie with sensitivity on full throttle said 'that means somebody will have to pound a stake through his heart' at this Janet sobbed and fled to the bathroom closely followed by Maggie, who paused long enough to fix Stevie one of her icy stares.

He looked at Sonny and me and asked 'What are you looking at me like that for? I'm telling you the truth; I've read all of Sanny's comics. We canny just batter his head in or strangle him or anything we really do need to make a stake and pound it through his heart' Neither of us answered him because we knew it was true, we wouldn't have blurted it out like him but that didn't make it untrue.

Maggie and Janet returned the latter still sniffling and wiping at her nose with some of my ma's toilet roll. Maggie had used the few minutes to come up with a plan. 'Tommy is bound to either try again to get into his own house or try some of his pals. We canny let him get to anybody tonight 'because that will just make him stronger and then tomorrow we will have more of them to find. We need to find him pronto, Janet is going home and if he comes back there she will hang a big white bath towel out of her windae so keep watching her windae and if you see a towel bolt ower there'

Stevie interrupted 'We need to all get crosses and some garlic' he urged.

'It's half past ten on a Sunday night in the Gorbals Stevie the garlic and Crucifix shop is shut' I said. He grinned at me 'Or holy water that would help, if the Crucifix and garlic shop is shut maybe the holy water shop will still be open'

Janet sniffed loudly and said 'I've got this and another two Crucifixes in the house so two of you can have one of them each' as she pulled a little cross from the neck of her t-shirt.

Maggie added 'I've got two as well so that's us sorted for crosses'

Sonny piped up 'I know here we can get garlic'

'Aye so do I, France' was Stevie's reply, but only because I couldn't remember where it came from in time.

'Have any of you actually seen garlic. What is it?' I asked.

'It's a ring of flowers' Janet said

'Naw it's no that's a garland' I said.

'I seen it in a horror film it looks like a wee white onion and it does come on a string you sometimes see French guys on bikes with a string of them round their necks' Stevie answered.

'When did you ever see a French guy in the Gorbals you warmer?' I asked him.

'Oan the telly ya dobber' he answered.

'They use it a lot down the Tandoori Mahal' Sonny said 'I thought we could ask them for some'

'Good thinking Sonny, do the Chinky's use it as well?' I asked.

Sonny shrugged his shoulders and spoke to Maggie 'You are never out of the pineapple why don't you ask the old happy slapper for some holy water'

'Don't be so disrespectful Sonny, it's the chapel no' the pineapple and Father Hunter is a nice old boy, it's nice he's still so enthusiastic. What would I tell him I wanted it for, it's no' as if I can say I'm conducting a mass is it? Maggie asked him.

'Tell him you want it to wash some sins away from Tam the Scam cause he's a proddy hanging about with wee fenian lassies, tell old Hunter you think you can convert Tam and he will probably give you a bath-full of holy water' Stevie suggested.

'There's holy water in the font Maggie and usually some in them wee bowls at the door what are they called again?' Janet said.

'Stoup's Janet but we can't steal holy water it wouldn't be holy anymore. We can ask father Hunter for some for Janet's ma and some for us because we need it. If he asks what for then we either tell him everything or nothing, if we lie to him the holy water will be useless anyway' Maggie answered, she was now our twelve year old expert on vampires, Catholicism and divinity.

'Ok let's get going and catch us a vampire' I said.

'There's something else we need' Janet said dismally. When none of us said anything she said it herself 'a stake'

'We need more than one' Maggie said 'We need one each. Janet this isn't for Tommy. He's gone; we need to kill the thing that is using him to release his spirit and let him rest in peace and go to heaven'

'She's right' Sonny told Janet and put his arm round her shoulder.

'You know she is' I said patting her arm.

Stevie followed our lead and tried to comfort her 'listen Janet the minute we pound that stake through his heart you will see his face become all peaceful. He will scream like a banshee at first but does become all peaceful after that'

We split up and went in two different directions, Stevie and Sonny went with Janet to her house to pick up her spare crucifixes and something to make into stakes. She had told them her maw had a few brush poles in the press that she wouldn't miss; they were going to sharpen them. Maggie and I headed to her house, to find her spare crucifix and whatever we could use as weapons.

It wasn't going to be so easy particularly with the way her Ma greeted us 'where's my bag of papers?' she was drunk.

I presumed she meant the vampire chronicles we had been looking through and left in my ma's house. Maggie jumped in to the rescue

'They're under my bed, I was reading them, I'll put them back tomorrow' she said.

'Why?' she asked Maggie 'Why were you reading them why now?' this was our chance to tell an adult. An adult that would possibly even believe us, one of the very few, or more precisely the only one.

Maggie didn't take the chance 'I wanted to see if there was anything about my dad in it'

'Naw you didnae, you've read all the papers before there's nothing about your dad in them. You know everything that's in them' she said glancing at me, perhaps embarrassed that I might have read them.

'Is this anything to do with wee Tommy going missing?' she asked again glancing at me wondering how much I knew. Maggie cut her short 'Naw ma wee Tommy has got nothing to do with your fantasies, come on Tam let's go' we walked towards her front door and heard her ma go into the living room. Maggie nicked into her room and came out with a cross on a chain and two hockey sticks, she handed me the sticks and pulled me out of the house in a hurry.

'Are we going to play hockey?' I asked.

'Naw make them into stakes, just bang them off the wall over there and half them in two' she said pointing to a low brick wall opposite her front door. I did what she suggested and within minutes had two jagged pieces of hockey stick which would do the job nicely if we met up with any vampires.

'Are you sure about all of this Maggie?' I asked and sat down on the wall. She sat down beside me.

'How do we know there even is a vampire? How do we know that Tommy is a vampire? What if we see him and stick one of these jolly hockey sticks in him and he starts greeting. What age is he? Eight? Ten? And you think one of us can stick this in his heart? Because of what? Because your ma has got a bag of junk under the bed about something that happened in nineteen canteen?' I said nervously, I didn't want to call her a liar or make out she was stupid, I liked her. But there was no way I was sticking broken stick into any wee boy. Maggie did something that I had never seen her do before and have never seen her do since, she cried.

I learned from Sonny and I put my arm around her shoulder 'Maggie I'm not slagging you, I'm just not positive that this is really happening. We haven't got any proof have we? What proof have we actually got? Janet said he was crawling up a wall fifteen flights up how does that work? Don't get me wrong Janet's your pal and she's alright most of the time. But maybe she's just been dreaming, maybe she fell asleep on her bed and dreamed about it. We don't know do we? I canny attack a wee boy because Janet had too much cheese on her toast Maggie and neither can you'

She sat closer to me and said 'I know I'm right I am and so do you, if Tommy or the main man turn up at any time we will know won't we?'

I could only say 'I hope so'

She sat up straight with a jolt 'Look' she said pointing upward. There was a big white towel fluttering from Janet's bedroom window.

'What do we do?' I asked Maggie. I was already moving towards the lifts, hopefully they would be working I didn't fancy climbing 15 floors to Janet's house. And anyway by the time we did that the vampire could have died of natural causes.

'Wait' she said and as she did I saw something above her falling and heading straight for her. I grabbed with both arms and threw both of us over the wall and onto a grassy embankment. We rolled a few feet in a tangle of arms and legs and finished up with me lying on top of her in a compromising position. We both reddened and rolled away from each other quickly. When we walked up the embankment to where we had been stood, we saw embedded between the bricks on the wall in an upright position, the broken shaft of a baseball bat precisely where Maggie had been sitting. If I hadn't moved her it would have gone straight through her. I looked at it quivering and noticed that there was blood on it, at the sharp end.

Stevie came bolting out from the stairwell, 'did you see him come out? He shouted at us, looking behind him at the lift doors which were closed and hadn't opened whilst we were sat there.

'See who?' I asked.

'Tommy' Stevie said breathlessly 'He came back to Janet's windae, I seen him Tam'

I waited a few seconds for him to continue he didn't he was looking back in at the lifts 'And what happened for fuck sake?' I asked aggressively, and no wonder how could he leave us hanging like that?

'Oh aye, he's definitely a vampire Tam. At first he just looked like a poor wee soul all white as a sheet and lost. He was tip tapping on the windae with his fingertips no' with his knuckles, it was like he didnae want to be too loud. Janet opened the curtains and he saw her and started to moan about how cauld he was and how he was missing his am and how Janet was being a rotter for no' letting him in. He actually said that 'a rotter' Stevie paused again to catch his breath and still he was looking over his shoulder.

'What are you looking for and what happened up there' Maggie asked.

'I'm looking for him, Tommy. You won't believe it but when Tommy was moaning about how cauld he was Janet just went and let him in. Me and Sonny freaked. But then I saw what she was trying to do, when she told him to come in she had one hand on her crucifix and one hand behind her back holding a stake we made out of a brush pole. Maggie looked at the broken baseball bat imbedded where we had been sitting moments previously.

'Naw that one's mine' The second Janet said he could come in he flew right in there on top of her, she barely managed to get the crucifix up on time but she did and it burned right into his cheek. I could see the shape of a wee Jesus on his skin like a black tattoo. He screamed like a scalded cat, there was a flash and he flew back against the wall. His face was pure evil Tam; he looked like a wee demon or something. He stared at me and then glanced at Sonny; I think he was deciding which one of us he could get at. I had my crucifix on a chain round my neck and took it out and let it hang down on my chest. Janet didn't have a chain on the other one so Sonny put it in his back pocket, a fat lot of use it was in there, as far as I know vampires don't bite you on the arse.

 He flew straight at Sonny, there was no way me or Janet could get to him on time so I did something daft. I threw my stake at him like a spear. It missed him and stuck in Sonny's arm' he said grinning.

'So how come it's down here' I asked.

Stevie grinned again 'Sonny pulled it out of his arm and threw it at me' he said and laughed.

'What are you two eejits all about, fighting with each other? Where was Tommy whilst you two were being stupit?' Maggie asked him incredulous at what she was hearing.

'I'm trying to tell you so if you two can shut it for a wee minute and let me finish eh? So Tommy's all for giving Sonny his first ever love bite. I chuck the spear at him miss Tommy hit Sonny. Janet throws herself in front of Sonny trying to get Tommy another good one with the crucifix. Tommy bolts out the bedroom door, and then Sonny takes the huff and chucks the baseball bat back at me. It goes out the window and by the looks of it nearly turns one of you two into a kebab. Tommy meanwhile flies into the living room; I don't mean actually flies by the way. He breenges into the living room and tries to bite his maws neck. Can you imagine that, he tries to kill his fuckin maw? She's lying out for the count in front of the telly with a three quarter's empty bottle of vodka on the carpet in front of her. Janet gets in the living room as tommy goes at his ma's neck like an Alsatian dug with a ham bone. But Tommy almost does a back somersault getting away from her, not only has she got on a crucifix but she's also got on a saint Christopher medal. And a pendant thing with a picture of the Celtic team that won the European cup. Now I don't know if the pendant made any difference but I don't think it did any harm. Do you know what I mean?'

'Where did Tommy go' I asked.

'Oh aye, right well when Janet goes for him he just crashes right out of the living room windae. I boogie over to the window and see him crawling down the wall like a four legged lift and scarper down here. End of story'

'So he could be in the flats somewhere then' Maggie says and then shouts 'My ma' and starts running up the stairs. I follow her thinking. Why the fuck does nobody want to use the lifts, they're working so why is everybody running up and down stairs. But I still followed her up to the third floor.

We can hear a commotion in Maggie's house; her front door is wide open. Maggie is at least four inches shorter than me and a stone lighter. If she turns sideways you can hardly see her. But she has the heart of a lion and some. She was through the door before me and ready to do battle, her 'hockey stick' was in her right hand and she meant to use it. The commotion was in her living room, and the sight we saw when we entered will stay hard wired on my retinas forever. Her ma was standing just inside the room with her back to the door chanting something in Latin and throwing water at Tommy from some sort of sprinkler thing. I later find out it's called an aspergillum, cool word. And it's normally used to sprinkle holy water during a mass.

 Tommy was crawling frantically back and forth across the ceiling; every time the water hits him it tears a strip from his flesh. As if she is whipping him with a cat of nine tails or something. He's frantic, he's scurrying across the ceiling from corner to corner, his face is filled with an expression of pure evil, and it isn't the face of an eight year old boy. It is older much older, and eight year old boy can't hate the way this thing was hating Maggie's maw. She just kept at it sprinkling him with holy water and it was weakening him, his efforts to escape were diminishing, he was wailing now each time the water tore a new line across his face or his legs. He still had parts of his school uniform on.

He was more devious than I had imagined his wailing and slowing down was a ruse, he took the opportunity of us opening the door to make a last dash for freedom. Maggie and her maw were too quick for him. Her maw sprinkled him again and again with holy water and he screamed Maggie went for him with the hockey stick and pierced his side. I was transfixed, I temporarily lost control of my thoughts, it was too surreal. A girl that I thought was probably girlfriend material and her strange maw were murdering a child in front of me and I was mentally cheering them on. How could this be happening?

'Kill him Tam' I heard Maggie scream.

Maggie's maw had forced Tommy into the corner nearest me and was lashing the holy water at him in a frenzy and shouting things at him in Latin. Tommy was beginning to smoulder and catch fire where the water was hitting him. He had torn the hockey stick from his side and discarded it. I still had mine in my hands. I knew I had to do this. This ridiculous and barbaric act, I had to kill a child. But he wasn't a child, he wasn't even human. I raised the sharpened hockey stick above my head ready to strike down. I would have done it, I could have done it and maybe I should have done it. I was too slow; before I could garner enough courage Maggie pushed past me and thrust her hockey stick clean through the heart of her best friend's eight year old brother.

And it was Janet's younger brother Tommy. The instant Maggie succeeded in pushing the stake through his heart whatever had been making Tommy into a monster left him. We could see his face settle into an angelic repose. His face became a countenance that would melt a thousand hearts at his upcoming funeral, an image that would adorn the front page of newspapers throughout Britain and spawn a million tears. They had killed Tommy. Maggie and her mad maw had killed an eight year old boy and I was at least a witness if not an accomplice. I ran.

I was fourteen years old what else could I do? I ran towards my house but halfway there I changed direction. My instinct had been to run home and tell my old man what had happened and he would sort it out. He was one of the good guys my dad; he was an electrician to trade and worked for the council on the subways. If anybody on our street had problems with anything electric they would chap our door and my old man would get to the bottom of it for them. The only thing was I don't think he was really my father. He was my dad, my da, my old man. Whatever you want to call him, he raised me and brought me up. He carried me over his shoulder once for over half a mile to the Royal Infirmary casualty department when I twisted my ankle playing peevers with Maggie and Janet. Just because he said it would be quicker than waiting for an ambulance. I was only seven and quite light but it still took a bit of doing and he did it. He came and watched me play for the school football team in primary seven and he agreed with me when I told him I didn't think I wanted to play football again because I wasn't very good at it. I had only played for the team because I was bigger than most eleven year olds. Being tall for my age didn't make me good at football.

So I know he was my dad, but I suspected he wasn't my father. I thought my father primary school headmaster Mr Macadam, but he wasn't always a teacher he used to be a priest, well he was when he got my ma pregnant. He was about fifty when I was born, my ma was fifteen. She always told me she is my was sixteen but I saw my birth certificate in the same envelope as her own certificate and also her marriage licence when I was looking in the biscuit tin on top of her wardrobe. I was looking for anything to do with my granda, my ma's da. He was in the Second World War and we were doing a school project about Dunkirk, my granny had mentioned Dunkirk to me once, telling me that my granda was there and told her it was a bunch of cowards running away, he wanted to stay and fight. But maybe that said more about him than anything else, he could start a fight in an empty room with his shadow, it even took cancer nearly two years to kill him in the end.

I don't know why I was even thinking about this, if I was going to tell anybody it would be my dad, not some ex-priest who must have taken advantage of my ma when she was only fourteen and left my dad to pick up the pieces. I read a book once about how pregnant teenagers were treated in Glasgow in the sixties, how sometimes they were sent to live in homes and their weans were taken off them. A lot of Glasgow lassies also sneaked away but my dad got together with my ma and married her on her sixteenth birthday to stop any of that happening to her. He was only a couple of years older than my ma so maybe he did have a wee fancy for her as well. But whatever way it was my dad sorted it out, so why was I sitting on the edge of the pavement wondering whether to go and see my dad or a virtual stranger who might or might not have given me my genes.

I sat there pondering my next move and looking down at the half broken hockey stick at my feet and was working myself into a mild panic when I heard someone approach me. I looked up warily and realised that I was probably too late to choose who to tell, the Gorbals Vampire was standing in front of me, smiling. 'Hello Tam the lamb come to the slaughter how's it hanging' He asked.

Chapter seven; my house 7th January 2015

Stevie P's flat is in Walmer Crescent in Glasgow, my house is in Waterside a small village on the north side of Kirkintilloch, a town which is approximately fifteen miles from Glasgow. I drove it in twelve minutes flat, I admit it was almost one o'clock in the morning and I admit I paid a thirty pounds fixed penalty for speeding through a camera but I still drove it in twelve minutes.

June was in the garden with three neighbours, two from the house on our right and one from the house on our left. She ran to me as I got out of the car, she had her house coat wrapped round her and slippers on her feet.

'Oh Tam I was so scared, where have you been?' she said hugging me and holding on for dear life.

'It's okay, I'm here, what happened? You're shaking actually shaking' I said 'What the fuck happened?' I looked over her shoulder at my next door neighbour on the right, Charlie Watson and he was smiling.

'She said she saw a rat Tam' he smiled again, the prick.

'There's no rats about here, nobody's saw a rat about here for twenty years or more' he said, the supercilious prick. 'It was probably a mouse and oh aye she also said your bath was full of spiders' He added and raised his eyebrows in a gesture meant to convey my wife was full of shit. The prick.

'Come inside hen' I said to June. 'Thanks for Your help Charlie' I said to the prick.

 His wife tugged at his sleeve, perhaps she picked up my sarcasm because he didn't

'No problem Tam, that's what neighbours are for, don't worry about it' he said and went back into his perfect wee house with his perfect wee wife to sit on his perfect wee couch. The prick.

My neighbour on the other side William Torrance said 'If you need anything Tam chap the door and don't worry about that prick. He's no worth bothering about' I just nodded and gave him the thumbs up. 'Come on hen, in the house' I said again to June and wasn't surprised when I didn't get away with it for a second time.

'Stop being so bloody condescending, I'm not going back into that house until we get a pest controller out here' she said and took my car keys from my hand and opened the car. She pitched me my keys and said 'lock that door and come sit in the car'

I did as I was told and joined her in the car, she had her arms folded across her chest and was scratching the upper parts of both of her arms, I could see red marks on her skin.

'I took a hold of one of her hands, if for nothing else just to stop her scratching and asked 'What happened'. She went very pale and said 'you can't tell anybody about this Tam and I mean anybody. This really happened. If it didn't happen then I might need sectioned' She withdrew her hand from mine and started scratching again. I said 'don't June' held her hand again and nodded towards her arms. She looked at the scratches and blanched, she looked terrified.

I asked again 'what exactly happened June, tell me everything.

She looked at me; I don't know what she was looking for. Maybe she was deciding whether she could trust me or not. She made me feel guilty. But guilty or not I would not be sharing my latest problems with her concerning the Gorbals vampire or Roderick Fitzgerald Murray as we now knew him. She started to talk softly I practically had to hold my breath to hear her.

'I have been seeing spiders all day. I know we live in the country and we get house spiders, but it's January Tam and we generally get fewer in the winter than we do in the summer, Because there's no' much for them to feed on is there?'

I knew she had a slight phobia about spiders, but it was only slight. It basically amounted to her telling me to get rid of them when any appeared, but as far as I knew they didn't normally give her the heebie jeebies.

'I thought it was strange but no biggie, but they were starting to bother me and make me feel itchy and not just that I was having a weird feeling that they were malignant. That somehow they were following me about the house and watching me or something'

I raised my eyebrows. 'I know, I know' she said and shrugged her shoulders. 'Tam this is the strangest night of my life, don't make a fool of me okay, just believe me I'm not lying to you' she said with a solemnity I recognised. June had a way of speaking to me when she that made it clear that my sarcasm and desire to say something funny were not appreciated or required. I nodded my acceptance that this was such a time.

'I decided to run myself a bath, I thought about phoning you to come home but I knew you and the boys would be enjoying Stevie's bachelor pad and I didn't want to spoil your fun. You've been a bit pre-occupied since after Christmas' she said touching my cheek. 'Anyway I lit some candles and started running the bath quite slow. By the way you need to turn the pressure up on that boiler; the water's taking a while to heat up'

I smiled to myself, she was getting back to normal but the look in her eyes wasn't normal as she told me what had happened. 'I put some bubbles in and got undressed and as usual the sound of running water made me need a pee. I sat down and waited the minute or two for my plumbing to start work and my thigh started feeling itchy. I scratched it and then it felt itchy again, and then I felt a wee sharp scratch on my thigh. I stood up and looked in the pan and there was a wet black manky rat staring up at me'

She retched as she told me this and her eyes filled with tears. 'It had bit me or scratched me Tam. I stood there staring at it and peed down my legs. Tam, I have never been so frightened in my entire life' She paused and gathered her thoughts, as she did so she tightened her grip on my hand, I could feel her nails digging in to my palm.

'Tam, I don't know how the next thing could have happened and I am scared it didn't. I am sacred that it did but I am more scared that it didn't. Because if it didn't then I have just had an hallucination and I need help' she hesitated again and put her head down and told me 'The bath filled with spiders Tam. I mean filled up until they were falling over the side and running across my feet. How could that happen Tam? Am I mad? Do you think I'm mad Tam? Do you?' she was frantic now and panicking and no wonder. As awkward as it was with us sitting in the front seats of the car I pulled her close and hugged her 'You're not mad'

As I held her I glanced down and noticed a trickle of blood on her thigh 'we need to get you to hospital you have been bitten' I said and reached to wipe the blood with my fingers. As I did a spider ran from under her nightgown and down her leg before falling to the carpet and then another and then another. She started slapping at her thighs and screaming, I was trying to hold her and calm her but it was impossible she was becoming more hysterical by the second. I got out of the car intending to go to the passenger side to try and help her, but before I could she was out of the car.

She was running in circles on the tiny patch of front lawn in front of our house, she was beating frantically at her head and screaming. I grabbed hold of her and tried to calm her but it was like wrestling with an eel. Mrs Torrance, our neighbour on the left hand side emerged with a tartan blanket which I attempted to wrap round June. Willie Torrance emerged with the news that he had called for an ambulance. Charlie Watson's contribution was a hungry stare from behind his curtain. It would be easy to believe that he had already begun to compose his gossip to share with his like-minded friends in the village. The prick.

I could hear a siren in the distance and was getting a bit more control of June, but I still considered taking the time to ask Charlie if a tall baldy guy who answered to the name of Roddy or Roderick Murray should turn up looking for me. Would it be too much to ask for Charlie to invite him in and give him a drink until I came back? I wish I had, Stevie P might still be alive if I had.

The Para-medics soothed June and managed to get her in the ambulance, they told me they were going to the Royal Infirmary and that I could get in the ambulance with June if I wanted, but I opted to follow them in my car, thinking I would need it to get us home in the morning. I called Sonny who was still at Stevie's flat to fill him in on what had happened. He told me him and Janet would join me at the hospital and Stevie and Maggie would go to my house and find out what happened. I laughed ironically and told him to tell them that the door was open but to watch out for spiders and rats.

The little scratch on her thigh turned out to be nothing much but she was still extremely distressed and after an initial psychiatric examination the resident psychiatrist suggested that she voluntarily sign herself in for further assessment. The alternative to this was that she would be sectioned, both June and I agreed that she would voluntarily undertake any examinations required. I knew there was nothing wrong with her mental health; Roderick Fitzgerald Murray had targeted her to get at me. He may not have realised it yet but that was a monumentally bad mistake.

Sonny and Janet found me in a family waiting room outside the psychiatric assessment unit. Janet had bullied the receptionist at accident and emergency until she had found out where we were. Janet had an *'Asda, bag for life'* stuffed with women's pyjama's and toiletries for June.

'I guessed you would have left the house in a hurry, and this place is bad enough without having to wear the ridiculous gowns they give you' Janet said softly.

I didn't look up, I just held out my hand for her to hold, I couldn't look up there was a pressure valve somewhere keeping my anger in check and my tears from flowing, if I looked up that valve might blow. Janet stood beside me and held my hand; Sonny shuffled to my other side and took my other hand in both of his. I was looking at his brown brogues at the bottom of his brown cords when I realised that we had been in this room before. Sonny's wife Sylvia had been brought here the first time she attempted suicide.

She had bit through the main vein in her wrist and had only survived because a parcel courier delivering to a neighbour's house saw her through her living room window walking around chewing on her arm and the resultant arterial spray when she succeeded in severing the vein. He had kicked her front door in and stemmed the flow of blood with a tea towel all the while struggling with Sylvia she tried to bite him

Sylvia was sectioned for eleven months following that episode and I had sat in this room with Sonny as the resident psychiatrist an impossibly young girl had explained to him that Sylvia was a paranoid schizophrenic currently suffering from severe delusions. She insisted that she was a vampire and that Sonny had been keeping her prisoner as a means of keeping the animals and children of their neighbourhood safe. She wasn't a vampire; we knew that, because when she first started insisting that she was, we checked. She had no aversion to holy water or the crucifix or daylight, we felt slightly embarrassed at checking, but we knew the reality, we knew that vampires were the real.

Sonny had relentlessly tried to get her help, initially from her GP, who proved worse than useless. Sonny got himself arrested for smacking the guy, he was admonished eventually which Sonny said was a vindication that the doctor deserved a smack and in fact probably deserved another one. After changing his GP the next one was more sympathetic but ultimately unable to help because Sylvia would come over all rational and deny any thoughts of being a vampire when confronted by anyone in authority. She would instead accuse Sonny and, on more than one occasion his friends, of trying to make her crazy as part of an elaborate plot to claim her insurance.

As I sat there with two of my closest friends holding my hands and thought of what this monster had done over the years. Starting with killing wee innocent Tommy, ruining all of our lives and destroying almost everyone we ever dared to love. My pressure valve gave up its losing battle. I stood up holding on to their hands 'Let's go kill this fucker for once and for all' both of their grips tightened on my hands and both of them nodded their agreement.

I smiled at both of them 'well you will need to let go of my hands we can't all get through the door at the same time' I said and Janet giggled, good girl.

Stevie called my mobile twenty minutes after we left the hospital and about ten minutes before we would reach my house.

'You know he's been in your house don't you Tam?' he asked and then told me how he knew. 'There's a putrid smell, like a sewer has burst, unless you've left your underwear under the bed for a while, it's safe to assume that the smell is from him. Maggie has found a load of dead and dying rats down at the bottom of your back garden. Some of them have had their heads bitten off and the blood sucked from them. There's no sign of any spiders, half a dozen on the bathroom floor maybe that look as if they have been stood on, but no major infestations. By the way who is the fanny hiding behind his curtains watching everything we do?'

I told him it was Charlie Watson and that his instincts were correct, he was a fanny but just ignore him, he's a gossipy old woman type of fanny and harmless really. He continued telling me about the condition of my house and garden, we were now approaching the bottom end of Kirkintilloch and were less than five minutes from my house.

'Where's Maggie now?' I asked.

'I'm not sure, she was here a minute ago' he replied and then said 'Oh for fuck sake Tam, she's on your roof, the bastard just came out of nowhere and grabbed her and jumped onto your fucking roof, I'm gonnae kill this fucker right here right now. I heard his mobile land on the ground and Maggie scream 'No Stevie don't' and then there was a crunching sound as if someone had stood on the phone and then nothing. Sonny drove my car onto my drive one minute later. All three of us raced round the back of my house and all three of us wished we hadn't.

Stevie was pinned to the back wall of my house in a crucifix position. He had been pinned to the wall using the solar lights that ran the length of my garden they were black and round and each of them had a spike at the bottom to hold them into the ground. He had one through each hand, one through his feet which were overlapping, and one through his forehead. The one through his forehead had some trailing weeds attached which almost created a thorn of crowns to complete the vision in front of us. The lights glowed weakly but we could still see that his throat had been torn open.

Janet sat down with a thud on a garden chair; she was clearly struggling to comprehend what she was looking at. As were Sonny and I. This couldn't be happening; we were supposed to kill him. We were supposed to kill this guy, whose name we had just discovered. Our plan was to kill him decapitate him, chop off his limbs and stuff all of his orifices with garlic. That was our plan; Stevie's plan because that's what Stephen King suggested was the proper disposal method for vampires.

 But our plan didn't include any of us dying so this just could not be happening, it couldn't and it wasn't, I refused to believe. Until Janet said 'Where's Maggie'

We all looked round expecting her to appear and tell us that she was okay and Stevie was going to be okay, because that was her fucking job, where the fuck was she. Sonny spotted her first, well he spotted something down the side of my shed that looked like clothing.

We walked slowly towards this bundle of rags and spotted it was Maggie fairly quickly; I dropped to my knees and began sobbing. She was basically bent double and crammed into a space that it would be difficult to cram a six year old child into. Sonny wasn't as weak as me he went straight to her and started easing her out of the space and as soon as he did she started swearing and shouting.

'Where have you lot been, what kept you. That bastard dragged me up onto the roof and then jumped down with me under his arm and stuffed me in that wee space. I could hear Stevie having a go at him and then I heard your car on your drive, where's Stevie?' she asked when she eventually noticed that he wasn't there. Sonny and I were in front of her, blocking her view of my house, we slowly moved apart and revealed Stevie to her.

Her hand went slowly to her mouth, she looked at me for confirmation that he was dead, I had no need to nod, she seen it in my eyes, my face my soul. 'It was his time' was all she said.

'No it fuckin wasn't' I said 'it wasn't his time it wasn't Tommy's time, it wasn't Sylvia's time it wasn't your ma's time, it wasn't the priests time it was nobody's fucking time. Roderick Murray has killed my fucking friend and I mean to eat his cold bloodless fuckin heart'

Janet said 'Amen' I loved Janet at that moment.

We had no choice but to call the police and leave Stevie where he was, nosey neighbour Charlie Watson would be our ally in that regard. Stevie was dead before we arrived at my house, so at least we couldn't be held culpable in that regard. The village of Waterside had probably never seen anything like the scenes that enveloped it over the next few hours. Charlie filled me in a few days later that he had counted twenty two police vehicles arrive in the village and over sixty police officers. I had to move out of my house because it was considered a crime scene. We were all interviewed under caution and advised to seek legal representation. The police team investigating the case included a detective inspector Helen Simpson; I had last encountered DI Simpson in 1994 when both my second wife and DI Simpson's colleague had been killed by Roderick Murray. Unfortunately for me both deaths had been recorded as sudden adult death syndrome and DI Simpson still blamed me.

'Well, well, well. Look what the cat dragged in' DI Simpson chuckled as she sat opposite me in interview room number four in Kirkintilloch police station. I nodded in return.

She sat down and leafed through a folder which was on the desk in front of her 'The officers in attendance tell me you had very little to say about what happened at your house tonight Thomas' she said putting the folder down and clasping her hands in front of her on the desk. 'But you never were the talkative type were you?' I still said nothing proving her point for her.

'Thomas, you are in deep shit this time my little vampire hunter. Oh yes, I know, I read all of Detective sergeant Newton's notes following her death in 1994. She had you tagged as a sort of cult leader dragging your mentally challenged buddies along on a journey into the depths of your deranged mind. Her notes over the last few days of her life indicated that she was closing in on information that would put you in the frame for more than one or two murders Thomas; according to her it's likely that you started your killing spree when you were about eleven or twelve. Does the name Tommy Jackson ring any bells?' She paused probably to give me a chance to protest, I declined the opportunity.

'Of course it does, Tommy was Janet's wee brother, and he went missing in 1974 as you well know. He was never found Thomas, that's highly unusual in itself. Despite what you might think very very few children go missing that are never found. In the last 100 years in Glasgow there have been two and one of them was wee Tommy Jackson. Since 1974 Thomas would you like to hazard a guess how many times your name has come up as part of a murder investigation? Go on have a guess, start at seven and keep counting, I will tell you when to stop. Okay times up it was eleven Thomas including your wee junkie pal we just scraped off the wall of your house it's now twelve' I flinched, she spotted it.

'Hmm now what forced a reaction from you Thomas, was it reaching the round dozen or me talking about your bisexual drug addled pal Stevie' she asked, hoping for a further reaction, she was disappointed.

Roderick Murray had once alluded to Stevie being gay now DI Simpson was doing the same. So what if he was, I felt sad that he had been unable to confide in us, actually more than that I felt angry that he hadn't. On that basis I decided that this was a ruse to get a reaction but why? Why would Simpson think that Stevie being gay would be a problem for me, it's 2015 for fuck sake who cares anymore.

She sat back and looked at me as if she had a chance of reading what was in my mind 'Why don't you want a lawyer, there's a fair chance I am going to be allowed to set up a task force to look into twelve murders all of which are related to you in some way. Do you think you are some kind of Hannibal Lecter or something? Do you want a movie made about you Thomas, is that it? Do you want to be famous or rather infamous? For that to happen you need to tell your story Thomas, you're a writer. A has been writer but still a writer. You know how it starts Thomas *once upon a time'* She got another reaction from me, a smile.

I appraised her and spoke 'have you fantasised about who will play you in the movie Helen? Do you wonder whether it will be a Hollywood star like Sandra Bullock or Scarlett Johansson or if they go all local it will need to be somebody from River City? Can I make a suggestion Helen?' she never answered so I made my suggestion. 'Why don't you get off your arse which is considerably wider than it was back in 1994 and find out who vandalised my house yesterday afternoon by filling it with rodents and spiders, terrorising my wife. And then start working out who murdered my best pal last night, instead of sitting their getting all damp thinking about meeting Brad Pitt' She very nearly slapped me again, the way she had during an interview in 94. But she recovered her cool just in time but not quickly enough for me to miss her fist clenching and unclenching.

'Are we done?' I asked belligerently.

'Oh no Thomas not by a long chalk. I have lots and lots of questions for you, let's start with how did you and Alexander Thompson manage to hold Steven Paterson up so high while the ladies were pounding metal spikes through his head and limbs' I smiled again and went back on silent running mode. She spent another three hours repeating absurd questions about everything from Tommy Jackson's whereabouts to whether Sylvia Thompson had really committed suicide or had Sonny and I helped her on her journey to the afterlife. I said nothing for those three hours nor did I react in anyway.

'I need a coffee, do you want anything Thomas, coffee, tea a lawyer?' she said trying to give the impression she could go on like this forever. I shook my head but then asked a question of my own

'How long can you hold me' it was her turn to smile at me and answer with a grin 'Quite a while Tam, quite a while' she slipped a sheet of paper out of her folder and placed it in front of me.

Apparently the police can detain you for up to twenty four hours as a minimum. They can then apply for extensions to that up to 96 hours in serious cases such as murder. Or even up to 14 days if you are suspected of terrorism. 'So 96 hours is the maximum then' I said to her as she sat down with her coffee and smug grin. 'Thomas, in these days of ISIS and terrorists in every suburb we at Strathclyde constabulary have to seriously consider whether the crucifixion of a Christian is an act of terrorism or not. At the moment I am plumping for the answer that it is. So you are with us for the full Bhoona, fourteen days. Think of it as a fortnight's holiday without the sun sand sea or sex. The good news is that the station canteen does a mean paella. So where were you on the 27th of December 1974, the day that Tommy Jackson went missing?'

She kept it up for another five hours before I gave in and asked for legal representation, maybe a lawyer could get me out of here in less than fourteen days. I was worried not only about June and my friends but about all of our extended families, Roderick Murray was out to punish us for his decades of agony.

The lawyer did his stuff I was released after seventeen hours, Janet and Sonny had been released after twelve hours, Charlie Watson's unequivocal statement that they and I had arrived after the horrific screams of Stevie Paterson which clearly signalled his murder had given the police no real option other than to let us go. I presumed the extra five hours of questioning me was just DI Simpson having fun. Maggie hadn't been released yet, we found out the next day that the police were reluctant to believe that she had been thrown from my roof landing down the side of my garden shed without sustaining any significant injury. An eye witness saw her being restrained on the roof by a shadowy figure and the same witness claimed that Maggie had been carried from the roof, not thrown.

The eye witness was Charlie Watson's wife, she was now under medication from her doctor because she also told the police that the man who held Maggie on the roof had appeared to walk down the wall of my house with Maggie under his arm kicking and screaming. They didn't believe her, particularly when Maggie laughed and showed them the bruises she had on her back from being forced between the shed and the garden fence.

We ended up back at Sonny's house licking our wounds and trying to console each other, but how could we. Stevie's death was too raw and too traumatic to handle with any degree of control. Janet wept openly and continuously into the early evening. Sonny sat by her side holding her hand in his and silently weeping. I walked to the local shops more than ten times on any excuse; I was desperate for something to happen, for Roderick to attack me. I would even have quite liked to get mugged; I daydreamed about taking out a couple of Neds and smashing their faces to a pulp. It didn't help, nothing could take Stevie's smiling face from my mind, nothing would stop the constant tam the bam, tam the sham, tam the lamb litany going around and around inside my head. I sat on a low stone wall and wept for my friend, after a few minutes someone sat beside me and held my hand I looked up through my veil of tears and saw Maggie. She said nothing I said nothing there was no need.

When we got back to Sonny's shortly afterwards Janet was cooking a pot of soup, she was peeling the layers from a ham haugh and dropping them into the pot. We all had the same thought at that moment whenever she had previously made this soup and Stevie had been there he would carefully ladle the soup into his bowl taking as many as the pieces of the ham as he could find. I briefly wondered if the rest of my life would be spent imagining what Stevie would say or do at any given moment. I have known grief, too much grief but never like this, I could feel my heart breaking. Stevie was the baby of the group not in years but in temperament, he wasn't the youngest but he had a Peter Pan quality that made him appear to be.

Maggie said to me very clearly 'Don't let this bastard break you Tam, we need you. Man up' I turned to tell her how that was an incredibly cruel thing that was to say to me, but she was talking to Janet at the sink. If she had said it then it was mind to mind, I suspected that it was me that had said it to me, because I wanted to believe that I was needed and I wanted to believe that I could man up. Well now was the time to find out, somebody was knocking on Sonny's window. We were three floors up in a tenement. We had been here before.

Chapter eight; 1974 the end game.

I stared at him and mulled his words over, 'Hello Tam the Lamb' how did he know my name, not just my name but my nickname? And what did he want with me, it couldn't be revenge I never actually touched wee Tommy. I looked over both of my shoulders, looking for a source of help I would accept it from anywhere, where were the Salvation Army when you actually needed them, it looked like the whole of the Gorbals in fact maybe the whole of Glasgow was empty. There was a pub less than fifty yards away from us, which normally would have people coming and going constantly, but not a soul moved in or out of it. I felt as if I was in a bubble and it was only me and him.

'Cat got your tongue Tam the spam' he almost made me smile there, I got it tongue and spam, both kinds of horrible cold meat the same as him really, that would have been beyond Stevie's sense of humour to think of.

I shook my head keeping as close an eye as I could on him, I moved the broken hockey stick nearer to my right side. This made him laugh and then move so quickly it seemed as if he had turned to dust and flowed past me. Before his laugh had died in the air he had swooped in seized the hockey stick and threw it in the air. He tossed it casually aside where, incredibly, it embedded itself in a lamp post. I don't know what force is required to skewer a metal pole with a piece of wood, or even if it is possible, but if it can be I would guess it's considerable.

I thought of my mum and how sad she would be when I turned up dead. She had high hopes for me and since I am an only child the wishes she had for me were practically the only ambitions she had. She obviously got on okay with my dad, well she didn't seem to have the black eyes or bruised cheeks that most of my friends mothers had at one time or another. But there was also a wee bit of my granda in me and if this freak wanted to fight then I would fight, I might not win but nobody wins all the time, at least I would go down fighting and hopefully hurt him in some way, maybe make him think twice about picking on young boys. But I must be honest as I stood looking at the hockey stick quivering I don't think I had ever been so scared in my short life. The thought that my entire life might only add up to a dozen years did occur to me, but I imagined my granda with his boxers pose, bent slightly forward fists raised to cover his chin, and thought 'okay big man let's do it'

He saw it in my eyes 'Oh master Thomas, your willingness to indulge in fisticuffs does you great honour but unfortunately to use one of your own phrases, you would be on to plums wee man. Should this proceed to a physical altercation I can and will tear you limb from limb with relative impunity'

'You and whose army?' I asked fists raised, ready to rumble.

'Delightful' he said, in his poofy voice 'I have chosen wisely, I have many armies to choose from Thomas. I can opt for the army of darkness' as he said this I saw fleeting shadows swirl behind him and to my side. I could almost make out people within the shadows, men with haunted faces and tortured souls, women with the agonies of time stretching their mouths wide in silent screams, children with tear tracks on their dirty faces and emptiness in their eyes. I knew that I could be joining them in their torment very soon.

'I could also opt for my nibbling gnawing biting scratching army' he said and four rats slithered out of a sewer grating and sat at his feet, quickly joined by six more emerged from a drain behind me and slithered across my feet, I only had sandshoes on so I could feel every claw trying to pierce my skin. One of them left a wee rat jobby on my toe, I was transfixed by it and wondered if he had such control that he could make it do that deliberately. I felt my skin crawl and imagined I could hear them preening their whiskers as they sat on their haunches on either side of him and joined him in staring at me. I imagined they were grinning.

'Chosen me for what you big poof?' I asked trying to gather my courage and show him I wasn't scared even though I was. I resorted to the language of my playground calling somebody a poof showed your contempt for them and showed that you were prepared to fight.

'Don't be like that Tam the scram' he said and smiled. I grinned inside at 'Tam the scram' because it was true, I had glanced to his side and tried to calculate my chances of making it to the pub, before deciding he would catch me before I made one step.

He smiled again, I felt as if he was almost reading my mind, he stared at me and I began to feel calmer all of a sudden as if a weight had been lifted from my shoulders'

'I need a go between, a facilitator, a can do sort of guy' he said sitting down on the wall where I had been sitting moments previously 'sit down, let's negotiate'

I moved as far along the wall away from him as I could, that made him smile, then laugh gently. He didn't seem so bad now, there was gentleness in that smile in fact there was almost love in his eyes.

'Mater Thomas I was about to say come closer I don't bite, but you would recognise that as a lie wouldn't you' he smiled again and then suddenly hissed and his eyes took on a reddish glow. I followed his gaze down to the crucifix around my neck and it was my turn to smile. I had almost been transfixed by his stare, but he had broken the spell.

'Well done Maggie mayhem, you were right about the crosses sweetheart' I said out loud, more to myself than him. 'So big man got a wee phobia about the catholic stuff then?' I asked with some amusement.

'Be very careful master Thomas, unless you have an abiding faith in those symbols then they become nothing, a piece of cheap tin fashioned in a crude shape, you are a man of absolute and unremitting faith Thomas aren't you?' he asked slyly.

'If you mean do I believe in the big man upstairs then that would be an aye pal' I said and touched the crucifix which lit up with a brilliant white light. 'Wow check out the batteries in that big man, and by the way I'm not a man of faith I'm only twelve, I'm a boy of faith I suppose, not even a teenager of faith yet'

'No Thomas, as you stand before me you are a man. It will make me sad to open your throat and slake my thirst. I had such exquisite plans for you; I would have offered you immortality to stand by my side through the ages to come. You would have had women that are too beautiful to behold directly, riches beyond counting and power beyond your ability to comprehend or even contemplate'

'Aye but would you have got me a game for Ranger's and a lifetime supply of *Irn bru*, you fanny' I laughed in his face; I had all the power I would ever need in a very thin silver chain around my neck. I was too young to know it then, but that power was in my heart and soul and I could have tapped into that bottomless reservoir without the need for a cross or holy water or any other symbol of faith, I had the pure faith of the young and inexperienced. I had not yet had the simplistic belief that everyone was basically good wrenched from me by experience.

'I'm away home now big man I'm a bit bored, but fair warning the next time I see you I won't be alone and I intend putting your lights out, permanently. I just watched one of my pal's kill her best pal's wee brother because you turned him into a monster for no other reason than that you wanted to. You shouldn't have done that, it was rotten and unnecessary. It just wasn't called for, if you need to eat people or drink their blood or do whatever it is you do then why not pick on some of the rotten bastards that are everywhere you look in this city instead of innocent wee boys who have nobody, including you, any harm.

Don't bother answering me, I already know what you would say, Tommy's blood tastes sweeter than some old slum landlord or crooked politicians would, doesn't it? Then I guess killing you like they weans did in 1954 will be sweet for me as well. See you later alligator' I said and walked away as nonchalantly as James Dean ever could have. I half expected him to answer 'in a while crocodile', but when I glanced over my shoulder he was gone. A solitary rat ran along the bottom of the wall where we had been sitting and slid bonelessly back into the drain it had emerged from.

I made my mind up that I had to confide in an adult, I couldn't carry this alone. I couldn't expose my dad to this monster. I also couldn't bear for him to think me deluded or stupid. I resolved to confront my biological father. I didn't care if he thought I was mental or daft, he was an ex-priest, he should know about this stuff and he had probably heard about the 1954 incident. It was the headmaster from the school he had taught at that had helped the police disperse the vampire hunting children back then. I knew where he lived; I had followed him home on my bike several times, considered introducing myself and spitting in his face. It was a house in Pollokshields and he had a wife and two children, both of them were younger than me. After he had used my ma, he had left the church and a couple of years later got married to a much younger woman.

I often wonder if his children knew they had a big brother. Of course they didn't he had manipulated and coerced a fifteen year old girl into bed and into pregnancy, it's highly unlikely he told them about the outcome of his wicked weakness.

My head was down and full of thoughts of brothers and sisters and fathers and mothers. So I didn't notice until the last second that someone had sneaked up behind me and grabbed my hand.

'It's done' Maggie said. I looked at her as if I couldn't understand the English language; it wasn't that I didn't know what she meant it was that I didn't want to know what she meant.

'Tommy's dead' she explained. 'And he's gone' I continued to stare at her wishing her to unsay what she was saying.

'Tam, my ma and me got rid of Tommy's body. It's better that way, there would be too many questions if we just left him lying somewhere' she said plaintively trying to get me to understand. I could only shake my head; I couldn't understand I refused to understand. I had watched her and her ma kill a wee boy and now she was telling me that they had hidden his body. I was already doubting my own senses, had he really been crawling across the ceiling. Had he really been screaming in agony and going on fire when he was struck with holy water.

'I am going to have to tell my father about this' I said to her and held her hand tighter.

'You can't Tam; they will send me and my ma to jail. Please don't tell anybody Tam please don't' she gripped my hand with both of hers as she pleaded. She looked into my eyes and probably for the first time but not the last I saw her strength and more than that I saw the strength of her love for me. Staring into those green eyes I also felt the strength of my love for her and young as I was I knew it was forever, come what may.

I nodded as if to agree to her request, but I knew inside that I had made my mind up. I needed serious help and my biological father was the only one who could provide it.

I didn't ask Maggie at that time what they had done with Tommy's body, I didn't want to know because if I did then I couldn't hide inside myself and pretend that I had nothing to do with Tommy's murder. I walked her home and followed her into her living room; her ma was sleeping on the couch oblivious to the debris around her. The broken furniture and smashed lamps that were the visible signs of the titanic struggle that she and her daughter had had with an eight year old boy. Maggie explained that she thought her ma was in shock and that's why she was sleeping. I said very little, I told her to keep her crucifix close and her ma closer and that I would see her the next day.

It was after midnight, the cold dark rain was falling incessantly, I stared from my bedroom window at deserted streets I decided that I couldn't really approach the priests house at that time of night. I sat in my room debating whether to tell my real da what was going on, or even telling my ma that I intended going to see her ex-priest. In the end I did neither, I drifted in and out of a restless sleep populated by screaming young boys that I chased with sharp sticks as I tried to avoid malevolent rats with sharp teeth.

At seven am the next morning I was sitting on my bike outside the priest's house on Albert Drive in Pollokshields it was quite a big house with a driveway and a garage. It must be well paid to be a headmaster or maybe he got a nice payoff from the Catholic Church when they defrocked him, if they did, or maybe they wanted him to just slither away quietly. He drove out of his drive and seen me standing at the edge of the pavement staring at him. He did what looked like a cartoon double take and almost crashed into a lamp post he swivelled his head that far round as he passed me.

He stopped and hesitated for a few seconds, no doubt wondering if he ignored me would I go away, eventually he reversed back to where I was still sitting on my bike and rolled his driver's side window down to speak to me.

'What do you want?' he asked glancing into the back seat where his children were sitting in their nice green blazers with the fancy gold emblem with some Latin words beneath it. But then their daddy knew a fair few Latin words didn't he.

'Help' I said and also glanced at his kids with a big smile on my face. His daughter returned the smile with interest, she was beautiful even with the gap in her front teeth, she had obviously just lost one of her baby teeth and it made her smile that much more sunny.

'Wait there' he said and abruptly drove away. It took him forty minutes to return. He slowed the car down and spoke to me gruffly.

'Come into the house, follow the drive round to the back of the house and come in that way.' I nodded nervously, perhaps had I been older and more sure of myself I would have made reference to the tradesman's entrance. As I wandered down the path marvelling at his huge back garden with the Wendy house, discarded bikes and fruit trees he opened the back door and ushered me inside, looking around nervously to see if any neighbours were watching.

'Have you had breakfast, my wife will be back in an hour but I could make you some toast or some cereal something' he enquired.

'I don't want anything to eat, I don't even want to be here but I need your help or at least your advice' I said, and asked 'do you know who I am?'

'Advice about what, did your mother send you or her husband' he said with suspicion and a large dollop of guilt writ large on his face.

By asking if my mother or her husband had sent me he had acknowledged that I was correct in my assumptions, he didn't ask if my father had sent me because he knew that he was my father. I wasn't sure where to start or how to answer him so I just blurted out what was in my head.

'No one sent me, I have a problem with a vampire and I want you to help me'

I expected ridicule or at least laughter, but he surprised me. 'What kind of trouble and who else knows about it?' he asked me with less belligerence in his voice than at any time since he had first seen me astride my bike at the front of his house. It seemed that he was more comfortable talking about a vampire problem than addressing who I was and his part in my creation

'Some of my friends know about it and one of their parents, he has already killed at least one person that I know of and has told me he will be killing me and all my friends, he wanted to make me some sort of servant to him I think. But when he realised that I believed in god and had power in my crucifix, he backed off. But he will be back and I want to kill him before he kills my friends or my family. Tell me how to do it' I said still standing just inside his kitchen door.

'Sit down' he said as he sat down at his old fashioned farmhouse type kitchen table it had six chairs around it and would have taken up most of the space in my living room, I don't think it would have fitted in my bedroom or my ma's kitchen at all. I sat.

'Can you help me; I don't mean you have to do anything I just mean tell me how to kill it. Maggie, my friend and her ma think it is the same vampire from back in 1954, do you know about him, where you there?' I asked.

He looked at me as if he was weighing up how much he could tell me, or maybe how stupid it would be to tell me anything at all. He again surprised me; he scratched his chin and paused for a few seconds before speaking gently.

'Thomas I don't know what your mother has told you about me. I am not a bad man, I was misguided and foolish and perhaps even self-absorbed. I didn't or couldn't think through the repercussions of what happened between your mother and me. What can I say to you, I loved your mother, with all of my heart. That love was adjudged to be wrong but it didn't feel wrong to me or to her. I paid a heavy price Thomas for giving in to that love' he said full of self-pity.

'Have you any idea how to kill this vampire or not?' I asked him straightforwardly and stood up as if to leave. I wasn't interested in his excuses or his attempts to induce empathy in me.

He grimaced slightly, perhaps he had realised how his whining and self-pity must be sounding. My mother was made pregnant by her parish priest when she was fourteen or just turned fifteen and he hadn't mentioned how difficult that must have been for her. He didn't mention how panic stricken she must have been when threatened with having the baby taken from her and put up for adoption to be raised by strangers. Or how scared she must have been when she first discovered her predicament and had to tell her parents. He mentioned nothing about her only the difficulties he had gone through. I turned to leave sickened by his self-indulgence and lack of care. He was clearly as weak now as when he seduced my mother.

'Sit down Thomas, I will tell you what I know' he said with a sigh, at least he had the sense to understand that I had no interest in his fall from grace. 'A group of schoolchildren back in 1954 cornered and killed a vampire, only a local police officer a headmaster and I knew about it. We decided amongst us to cover it up, it would do no one any good to imprison the eight or nine children who actually did it. The biggest majority of the children didn't actually know what was going on, they were merely the audience. I conducted a mass a few days after the incident above the tomb into which the children had thrown this vampire and the body parts they had hacked from him. The mass was unsuccessful; I abandoned the mass less than half way through with feelings of extreme nausea, and if you must know I lost control of my bowels as well. My faith and my commitment to my vow of celibacy were already in doubt by then, I carried on for ten more years but my abandonment of my faith was inevitable.

I wanted to scream at him that this wasn't about him, I needed real and practical help and all he had to offer was whimpering self-pity. He looked me in the eye and must have seen what I thought on my face 'Of course that's not what you need is it Thomas, a history lesson. You need help here and now. Well to answer your question bluntly, the church does not acknowledge the existence of vampires so have no rules or procedures on how to kill them, and the Catholic Church is nothing without rules and procedures. But I did a bit of research back in the sixties, to be honest I spoke to a few geriatric priests both here and back in the old country and they gave me the solution' he said with a grin of satisfaction as if he had just solved a cryptic crossword clue.

I looked at him with a raised eyebrow willing him to go on and get to the point.

'An exorcism is the answer' he said triumphantly. 'You take me to this vampire and I will perform an exorcism, I will send his dark and demonic soul back to hell where it belongs' I was thinking that he had seen the movie *'The Exorcist'* and he fancied a go at it himself, he actually looked pleased at the prospect, his eyes lit up. Maybe he could see personal redemption in this situation.

'So you will help me kill him then, just you and me, I can tell my pals to back off and stay out of it' I asked with palpable relief. I felt as if a load had been lifted. 'I think he may be at the Southern Necropolis' I suggested. He agreed 'that would make sense, he will be bound to that area, what if we agree to meet there this evening at sundown, which should be around four thirty, in fact we should meet at four so that we can spot him as he emerges'

'The southern Necropolis is a big place' I reminded him, 'How can we cover all of it on our own?' He again agreed and suggested that we would have to involve some of my friends if we were to be sure to find him. At every passing word from him my confidence in him was diminishing. But even I couldn't see an alternative to involving the others, there was no way I was involving my parents. I did suggest that he could contact the policeman and the headmaster that had been part of the cover up back in 1954, but the teacher was dead and the policeman now lived in Canada. So we settled on meeting at 4 pm and I would bring my four friends with me and we would kill a vampire together, or as he insisted exorcise a vampire, we could not kill that which was already dead. I left his house more scared than when I had first arrived; I was also profoundly disappointed in my mother's choice of father for me.

I had obviously dogged school that morning, well I could hardly get my ma to write a note to the teacher telling her I would be absent due to the fact that I had to go and see my defrocked priest of a father and discuss the best way to kill a vampire. I almost fell of my bike laughing at the look that would be on Miss Hunter's face if I had got my ma to write that.

I had to hide behind a bus stop at the school so none of the teachers would see me as I waited for Sonny and Stevie to trudge out with their heads down.

'Hey bum boys, who fancies a night in a graveyard' I said as I forced my bike in between them from behind.

'How were you no' at school' Sonny asked me, always playing the monitor.

'Who cares?' Stevie asked 'Is it a party? Have you knocked some vodka from your ma or something?' I looked at him uncomprehending.

'The night in a grave yard is it a party?' he explained.

'No, it's so that we can do some exorcising' both of them looked at me as if I was daft.

'No exercising, running and all that, I mean exorcising a vampire like in that film *The Exorcist* where that wee lassie was possessed with demons and the priests chased them out of her' they still looked at me as if I was daft.

Stevie spoke first 'Vampires aren't possessed with demon's they are the un-dead how do you exorcise the un-dead'

'Somebody I know told me that you could, and he should know' I said defensively, before they picked up on what I had said Sonny had his say. 'You canny just do an exorcism Tam, you need to be an ordained priest, you need to get permission from the Vatican and that can take months. There are all sorts of rituals and procedures you need to do before you even speak to the Vatican'

'How do you know all that you're no' even a Tim' Stevie asked Sonny.

'Stevie have you ever been to a library' Sonny asked him with intense seriousness.

'Aye, they used to take us there when were in primary one and two. Remember that old specky woman with the tights that were all stitched up with wool, reading us fairy tales like Hansel and Gretel and that' Stevie said with a happy grin.

'Well see when you sneaked a look through your fingers and saw all the square things on the shelves. They are called books and I read some about vampires and demons and shit like that, it's how come you learn things' Sonny said with his trademark sardonic smile.

'Ha ha, ya fanny' Stevie said in his own inimitable style.

Sonny looked at me and realised what I had said a few seconds earlier 'Who should know?' he asked me.

'Who should know what?' I asked playing for time.

'You just said that somebody told you that a Vampire could be exorcised and that he should know. So who is it that should know, have you been away seeing a priest' Sonny asked knowing that he was on the right track.

Stevie was perplexed, which was a semi-permanent state for him during his teenage years 'You're no' a Tim either Tam, I've two questions for you, why have you been seeing a priest anyway and did you keep your hands on your winkle, you know what they old bible bashers can be like' he laughed at his own joke, much more than it was due to be honest.

'I saw an ex-priest this morning' I told them and hesitated, I wasn't sure how much to tell them.

Sonny stared at me again, I always felt that Sonny was looking straight into my brain and discarding all the jokes and rubbish that I spoke and getting to the truth. I looked round, we had reached a wee swing park and I wheeled my bike in there and sat on one of the benches that were usually full of wee lassies looking after their wee brothers and sisters, whilst their ma's got the dinner ready for their men coming home.

Today we had the place to ourselves, I wondered if I was giving out some sort of signal to keep people away from me. If I was it wasn't affecting Stevie, if he had sat any closer to me on the bench we would have been wearing one pair of trousers between us. Sonny joined us on the bench, he was still staring at me, he knew I was hiding something and he looked as if he wasn't looking forward to finding out my secret.

'I went to see a priest this morning, well actually an ex-priest and he has agreed to help us stop this vampire. If we can get a grip of it somehow then the priest said he will carry out an exorcism on it.' I said deciding not to reveal who the priest was.

'This won't work Tam; somebody is gonny die if you try this shite. Forget the priest let's just get tooled up again with stakes and crucifixes and that and go do him in ourselves' Sonny said.

'Good idea Sonny, let's show this bastart who the *'young sooside cumbie'* are' Stevie said with bravado referring to one of the local gangs. Whoever the *'young sooside cumbie'* were it wisnae us.

'Stevie you don't half talk some shite son. Sonny this priest seems to know what he's on about and look at how this vampire fanny reacts to anything to do with the pineapple' I said trying to get sonny onside.

'Okay Tam you're the boss but I think this is mental and somebody is gonny die and if it's me then I will never talk to you again' Sonny joked and a minute or so later Stevie got the joke and laughed.

'What are you'se three dim wits laughing at now' Maggie asked as Janet and her climbed the fence and came into the swing park. I say climbed but the fence was only three feet high so they basically stepped over it. I found it slightly difficult to look at Maggie; I was amazed at how she could carry on as if nothing had happened. Then she looked directly at me and by the force of her will alone made me look into her eyes. They were no longer the eyes of a ten year old girl, they had seen too much. There would be no more dolls and prams for her, no more scrap books and skipping ropes, those days were gone. From this day forward there would be a life spent watching for vampires and being ready for them when they appeared.

Janet looked as if she was in shock, she told us her parents were still hoping against hope that her wee brother Tommy would turn up somehow. Janet of course knew that he couldn't, Maggie and her ma had killed him, and she was finding it incredibly difficult to listen to her ma and da telling each other that he would be fine, he would be home soon and everything would be alright.

'Janet we can't bring Tommy back but we can kill the bastart that took him, and we are going to, tonight' Sonny said trying to offer some consolation to her.

'Aye, us three are going with a priest to the necropolis and we are going to do him in' Stevie added passionately.

'Us four' Maggie insisted.

'Us five' Janet added through her tears.

So it was settled all five of us would meet at the gates of the southern necropolis at four o'clock half an hour before sundown. It would already be dark by that time, it was January in Glasgow, and real sunlight was restricted to about ten minutes a day. The rest of the time it's either dark or overcast, but overcast around here is virtually the same as dark. We have a propensity for producing dark clouds in Glasgow and not just in the sky.

I was first there, I always am. Maggie joined me within minutes.

'Where is everybody' she asked taking my arm and huddling up to me. I felt my face warm up.

'It's only a quarter to four, they will be here shortly' I mumbled, worried that Sonny and Stevie would turn up and see how close Maggie was standing to me. I thought about edging away but I didn't want to think I didn't like her and the truth was I was enjoying her being close. Before I could decide Stevie turned up but not alone, there were a group of about eight other children behind him aged from six to ten or thereabouts.

I grabbed him and pulled him aside, 'what the fuck are you doing, what do you think this is a fucking Sunday school picnic ya fanny'

At least he looked slightly embarrassed 'Sonny came back to my house after school earlier on and my wee cousin heard us talking about tonight, so what was I supposed to do. He threatened to tell my ma what we were doing if I didnae let him come along'

I shook my head, when in fact I wanted to shake him but said nothing more as I spotted the priests car pull up outside the gates of the graveyard. He got out of the car and approached me 'Thomas this is quite a little crowd you have here' as he said this Sonny Janet and another six or seven children sauntered around the corner some of them carrying what looked like weapons.

'For god's sake what the fuck is going on here?' I asked no one in particular.

'Don't blaspheme Thomas' the priest said with a smile. 'Let's get everyone inside the gates Thomas if anyone sees this gathering they will be very suspicious and most likely contact the police' he suggested.

We did as he advised and gathered in a crowd near one of the big gravestones and turned to him for guidance as he was the only adult there. He sized us up and down and told us his plan.

'I am sure that you all know why we are here, fantastic as it seems, we are indeed here to rub out a vampire. Rid the earth of an abomination, a lord of darkness, a servant of Satan, a demon in human form. Gather round I wish to perform a blessing that will keep you safe, this night. Safe from the vileness and evil of this thing we hunt this affront to humanity, this beast. This taker of souls, this child killer, this monstrosity.

 We huddled closer together, I thought that he could maybe let up on scaring the weans a wee bit, but looking round they all seemed to be getting pumped up by this guy. They were murmuring and looked anxious to get on with the fight. He took out some holy water and traced a cross on everybody's forehead one by one, and then gave everybody a wee bit of paper to eat. Maggie told me later it was called sacramental wafer and was supposed to represent the body of Christ, it tasted like paper to me. He was muttering something in Latin about dominos and sannies, he had put a silk scarf with tassels on it round his neck and he kept kissing that as he walked in amongst us. Some of the weans wiped their foreheads as soon as he looked away from them, they were more interested in getting on with the hunt, judging by the look of fervour in their eyes.

I heard a commotion outside the gates at the same time as I heard a loud roar of laughter coming from behind us; it was him, the vampire laughing. He approached us with a nonchalance that scared me, he could see the holy water in the priests hand and the number of people milling around with weapons. Okay they were all children but they were Glaswegian children with sharpened sticks, a variety of knifes and broken *Irn Bru* bottles, a not inconsiderable enemy.

'Father Macadam, or should I say ex-father Macadam, no I am wrong you are a different type of father now aren't you father, I mean daddy. You sullied the cloth you wore and couldn't resist fornicating with young Thomas's mother back in the day, what was wrong with you man, were there no altar boys that took your fancy. Was it really necessary to impregnate the virgin with your dirty seed' the vampire seemed to glide to within a few feet of the priest. When suddenly he did that trick of turning into a cloud of dust and smoke, which seemed to envelop the priest for a fraction of a second.

The vampire was now instantly facing the priest and in his hand he held the vial of holy water that the priest had used as part of his blessing. He raised the vial and looked closely at it and then smelled it and said 'A fine vintage daddy, 1974 I believe' and then drank it in one swallow. He laughed hysterically at this and pointed at the priest 'Look at his face Tam the lamb. That's what you are tonight Thomas, a lamb, a sacrificial lamb. This bogus man of god, this impostor has brought you to me as a sacrifice, to get rid of you. You are an embarrassment to him and a threat to his fragile marriage. What would Mrs Macadam think of his dirty little secret, his abandonment of his faith and his God? And how safe would she believe her daughter to be from this spoiler of children. He likes them fresh Tam the lamb, did you not see how he lingered over your sweetheart Maggie as he performed his bogus little mass. Couldn't take his eyes off her burgeoning little buds'

The priest exploded in a rage and threw himself at the monster crying out for his father to help him. His father proved as useless to him as the priest, my natural father, was to me. I couldn't tell how it happened but suddenly the vampire had a grip of the priest by the throat and was lifting him free of the ground and snarling at him 'How dare you threaten me with your false trinkets and dead God, you will burn in hell for eternity.

He then tossed him aside like an old jacket; he landed against a headstone with a thud. His eyes were open and staring at me, but there was no comprehension in them he was dead. The only adult there was dead. I looked around at the fifteen or twenty children that were there and they were mostly backing away. Not Maggie, Janet, Sonny and Stevie, they moved forward as one and stood by my side, two on either side of me.

'How sweet' the vampire laughed 'Now I can take you all out with a single sweep of my arm' He swept his arm across us but leapt back when Maggie swung her hand which was curled into a fist and holding her crucifix at him and made contact with his hand as it swept past her.

'Let's do him' Sonny said and leapt at the vampire with his improvised stake, which looked like the shaft of a road sweeper's shovel. The vampire was too quick for him and slid smoothly aside with a contemptuous laugh. He then made a quicker than lightening lunge at Maggie, which Stevie and I tried to intercept. But he fooled us by diverting his attention to Janet at the last second, and suddenly he had her, he was standing behind her with his mouth at her neck licking it.

'What now Tam the clam, have you got nothing to say to your wee fat bird before I make her mine?' he laughed and licked her neck again. Janet struggled but he tightened his one handed grip on the back of her neck and caressed her cheek with his other hand drawing a long nail down her jawline and under her chin and using it to push her head up so we could see her distress.

'Calm down my little podgy girl, you are about to experience ecstasy that your virginal friends can only dream off. We could see a trickle of blood run down her throat, his nail must have pierced the skin, and he licked this trail of blood. Perhaps it was his blood lust and excitement that momentarily distracted him or perhaps Sonny's distress added to his speed, But all at once Janet was on the ground and the vampire had a crucifix embedded in his left eye.

He let out a scream that could have wakened the dead, and perhaps it did. It certainly caused mayhem in the necropolis. I turned and saw a crowd of children which looked to be over a hundred or maybe even a couple of hundred strong streaming through the gate with weapons held aloft. That must have been the commotion I had heard when the vampire first turned up. I was torn, I was kind of proud to see a gang of Gorbals children once more prepared to enter where adults wouldn't and battle evil in its vilest form. But on the other hand sonny had put the vampire on the back foot and we had a chance to finish it off if we hurried after it and these kids didn't get in our way.

I grabbed a baseball bat from an eight year old girl as I passed her. I don't if it was her that had carved the handle of the bat into a spike but someone had. Sonny and I set after it with hate in our heart and vengeance in mind. The gang of kids whooped and yelled and followed us, as if we were two pied pipers enticing them to follow.

Sonny spotted it crouched behind a crypt, coincidentally it was the crypt of Alexander 'Greek' Thompson and our very own Sonny Thompson found him there. We stood and watched him scream and writhe around on the ground as he tried to dislodge the crucifix from his eye. I knew Sonny was strong, I had fought him enough times to realise that but I don't know where he had got the strength to embed a three inch sliver of silver into this monstrosity's eye, so deep that it couldn't be extracted even by a beast with superhuman strength.

We watched it for a few seconds before sonny said 'Do him Tam' and I did. I raised the baseball bat high above my head and brought it down with all the strength I possessed. But it wasn't only my strength that guided it straight into the thing's heart. I felt a multitude of hands on the bat and a heard a multitude of voices giving me purpose. A small hand closed over mine as I struck and a small voice told me 'thank you' as the shaft of the bat pierced the monster's heart. That small voice and small hand both belonged to Tommy Jackson; I felt his breath on my cheek and an angel's kiss as he moved on to somewhere better.

The thin at my feet started to dissolve into a cloud of dust and smoke and it slid down a drain at the sound of the path as we heard sirens approaching and saw blue lights flashing.

Extract from a newspaper report the following day.

The Daily Record

24th Jan 1974

Mystery at the Necropolis?

Police arrived at the southern Necropolis in the Gorbals area
Of Glasgow yesterday evening to find a dead priest and a crowd
of bloodthirsty children.
Speculation has begun linking the incident yesterday to the incident
in 1954 when 200 schoolchildren went on a 'vampire hunt' at the
very same location.
Police spokesman Superintendent Daniel Duffy laughed off any
supernatural element when he said 'John Macadam, the headmaster
of

Abbotsford primary school, who was formerly a priest of the same
parish
Was found dead in the Southern Necropolis, of a suspected heart
attack.
At the same approximate time several local children perhaps
numbering
between forty and fifty were indulging in what could only be called
a mock gang fight. No children were injured and any attempt to
connect
these two incidents and add a supernatural element is ridiculous.
This newspaper reserves the right to suspend its judgement until we
conduct
A vampire hunt of our own. Read this week's Sunday Mail to see what
we have
unearthed.

Chapter 9; 2015 revelations

Rap, rap, rap, three more gentle knocks on Sonny's kitchen window.
Janet and Maggie were still standing at the cooker consoling each

other and preparing a lovely pot of steaming hot vegetable soup because as Maggie had said, we had to eat; we would need all of our strength to get through the next few days, particularly if we were to complete our task of killing Roderick Fitzgerald Murray, the Gorbals vampire for a third and final time.

Sonny beat me to the window by a nano-second at most and tore the curtains back with such force that he ripped the curtain rail from the wall rawl-plugs and all. Two unknown faces hovered there and we could see their mouths moving, Sonny tore the window open almost taking it off its hinges.

'Aw right big man, gonna let me in for a wee minute it's fuckin freezing oot here man' the first face said with a look of abject misery. 'Goan big man just to I get my circulation gaun' the face said and laughed like a lunatic as the second face made it's plea 'Big Roddy said that youse were all brand new and widnae see us hanging about oot here, that youse would invite us in and give us a wee bit of subsidence'

Maggie had appeared between Sonny and I and threw water at both of the unfortunate creatures saying 'There is no sustenance here for you take yourself to the church and beg forgiveness from god there, seek redemption and saviour before it is too late' both pathetic creatures wailed and screamed as they fled. It was only then that I noticed that the water Maggie had thrown at them came from a small vial she held in her hand. I presumed correctly that it was holy water and watched as she tucked the bottle into her cardigan pocket.

I marvelled at our collective optimism. This fantastic four of middle aged has-beens with cardigans and slippers. With middle age spreads hanging over our waistbands and bags under our eyes, and aches and pains that multiplied when undertaking the arduous task of rising from a sofa.

What were we thinking of, how could we possibly go after a vampire, one of the un-dead with the strength of twenty men and the cunning of twenty foxes. In 1974 when we had been ten and twelve year old children we had got lucky, incredibly lucky. Our youth, enthusiasm and naiveté had won us the day. In 1994 when we were thirty-something's, we possessed the fitness, strength and fortitude to take on this mammoth task, maybe even the courage and determination to take on the world and its auntie. But we were in our fifties now. Sonny was probably as fit as he had ever been, albeit he had a slightly dodgy knee. Maggie was as slim and spry as she had been as an eighteen year old college student. I could possibly run (or fast walk) fifty yards without having an embolism or heart attack. Janet probably even less. The physically fittest of us all had been Stevie who claimed he still had a pair of *Levi 501's* that he had bought and worn when he was seventeen and I believed him. But despite his outer appearance of fitness and strength and his inner resolve, he was dead, he hadn't proved capable of standing up to our foe, our nemesis.

I am not normally given to despair; my lifelong friendships with these four people had given me an inner belief that everything would always be okay in the end. That people were intrinsically good and that light would conquer darkness as long as you had faith. No matter what life looked like at three o'clock in the morning, dawn was around the corner and things would look better then. Even if they weren't better at least they would look better and could be tackled. But losing one of the five of us had thrown me neck deep into the most hideous depths of despair that I had never experienced.

I couldn't erase from my mind's eye the image of Stevie pinned to the wall of my house. His throat ripped out and the blood stains on the wall below him. I struggled to find the strength within me to take up the cudgel again to rise and be the person I wanted to be. How could I, he died at my house, where I had sent him. I had dreaded this day since I had been twelve years old. I knew that someday I would bear the responsibility of the death of people I loved. Stevie wasn't the first of course, I had been responsible for the death of my second wife, and perhaps even the deaths of all of the people that Roderick Murray had killed since I had failed to end his existence in 1974 and then again in 1994.

I made my excuses and left the other three to their own devices and went to bed, I wasn't tired and couldn't possibly sleep. I needed to think, I had to take this responsibility I had been given when I was a twelve year old Gorbals boy seriously and work out a plan. A way to end Roderick Murray a way to absolve myself from the desperate guilt I was feeling. I felt guilt for every single person he had killed, and every single life he had ruined by taking their loved ones from them. I even felt guilty about something he had alluded to during a previous battle. He accused me of experimenting by tasting the blood of my first wife and he was correct, I had.

It happened without deliberation or forethought. She had been sitting on the sofa with a bowl of soapy water at her feet shaving her legs, watching *Coronation Street*. It was 1983 and the Deirdre, Mike Baldwin and Ken Barlow love triangle was at its height. I was only twenty one my first wife Patricia was even younger. It was during a scene where Ken Barlow pushed his wife Deirdre up against a door and screamed in her face about her affair with his love rival. My wife clearly got overwrought as she managed to cut a fairly deep gash into her shin with what was supposed to be a safety razor. I was sitting on the floor with my back against the sofa she was sitting on inches away from her legs and I unthinkingly leaned over and licked the oozing blood.

She made a sound of disgust and pulled her leg away, I got up and sat on the sofa beside her and apologised with some embarrassment.

She made another fainter sound of disgust and said 'that's really weird Tommy what are you some kind of vampire or something, do you think you're Count Dracula' and laughed.

I got angry and slapped her once on the side of her face and screamed at her 'don't you ever fucking call me that' She fled the house and went to her Mothers, whilst I was frozen to the sofa in mute disbelief at what I had done. While it was true that I had grown up in the Gorbals, which like most areas of Glasgow had it's more than fair share of domestic violence. It was not something I had experienced first-hand in my family.

 But it was something that I had witnessed on a weekly if not daily basis. When the pubs in the Gorbals came out on a Friday and Saturday night, it was commonplace to see a husband drag a wife home by her hair. Or slap punch or kick the same wife with impunity. I had more than once witnessed random acts of domestic violence where, when the police were called and turned up, the man was told to take his wife home and not to bring his troubles out on to the street. In other words domestic violence was to be kept behind closed doors it was not for public consumption. As long as it was kept behind those closed doors then no one need be any the wiser, out of sight out of mind was the official position.

When I was about sixteen I asked my parents about this condoning of violence against women, my mother told me that unfortunately some men communicated with their fists rather than their mouths.

A look passed between her and my da that made me think my house was perhaps not the sanctuary against violence that I thought it had been, but then my da gave his opinion that men who raised their hands to women were nothing more than cowards, whatever the provocation. He glanced at my mother as he said it, looking back now I think perhaps he had been making an apology to her for something he had done. Perhaps as I had, he had lashed out in anger and was now remorseful. I don't really know it was never discussed again. What I do know was that I never seen my da raise his voice against my mother let alone his hands.

I sat on the couch for many hours wrestling with my conscience and struggling to decide what I could do to apologise to Patricia and repair the damage I had caused. I also tore myself apart wondering if indeed I had a desire to be a vampire. Did I regret that I had worn a crucifix the night the Gorbals vampire had told me he wanted to make me immortal make me as powerful as he was. Should I have thrown the symbol of god aside and embraced everlasting existence, had I missed the only opportunity to live an endless life filled with power.

I lay on the floor the whole night selfishly crying because of what I had done. If my da found out he would consider me a coward, my mother would never look at me with affection again. I gave no thought to how I had made Patricia feel, none at all, and being only twenty one was a meagre and puerile excuse. I wrote her a letter full of self-pity about how bad I felt and how my parents would react if she told them and begged her forgiveness for a second chance.

To her enormous and eternal credit she didn't just ignore me as perhaps she should have she sent the letter back to me with only a few words written at the bottom 'I can't forgive you because then I would need to forgive my da and I can't do that Tommy, goodbye'.

Looking back now I can appreciate her candour and admire her courage, she moved away a couple of months later. She left Glasgow and moved to Birmingham, I was told by a mutual friend that she went there with a new boyfriend and by a closer friend that she had gone on her own, heartbroken at the breakdown of our marriage. I chose to believe the closer friend because I think Patricia had loved me and had felt the deepest sense of betrayal when I failed to be the man she thought I was, in fact failed to be the man I hoped I was.

As I lay in the bed attempting to put my past life in perspective and steeling myself for what I had to do next, I understood why I was thinking of Patricia Keenan, my first wife, and Julie Anne Chalmers my second wife. As well as Christina Newton the police officer killed in 1994 and all of the other victims of Roderick Murray. I was thinking of them because I was seeking absolution, I was trying to cleanse my soul. My intention was to seek out this monster and destroy him or die in the attempt. I needed the purity of innocence to fulfil my obligation of ridding this world of Roderick Fitzgerald Murray. He had terrorised the Gorbals for over a hundred years and his days were numbered. One of us was going to cease to be very soon, and I couldn't let it be me.

In the morning I spoke to Janet, I reminded her of the two old people she had been planning to speak to, the Davidson's or something. The parents of that woman, Mrs Lawrence, who cleaned up the necropolis and told her that her parents who were now in their nineties remembered some incidents around 1954 that pointed to a vampire being around the Gorbals at that time.

I suggested that after what had happened with Stevie that I should accompany her to this interview, that in fact none of us should spend any time alone whatsoever until we had resolved the problem of the vampire. I also asked Sonny and Maggie to revisit Sinead the former girlfriend of Stevie who worked with the homeless and find out if she had discerned any pattern in her clients that had gone missing, anything that could help us pin down where Murray's lair may be. We had to hunt him down, he would no doubt return periodically to try and destroy us when he could. But I wanted to take the fight to him not wait for him to bring it to us. The two Neds at Sonny's window the previous night were proof enough that he was around and still taunting us. I had to find a way to bring him to me in person.

Sonny and Maggie agreed to visit Sinead and Janet and I decided that there was no time like the present to visit the Davidson's. Janet telephoned Mrs Lawson and arranged to meet her at two that afternoon at the care home.

We sat in my car waiting for Mrs Lawrence, Janet cajoled me into phoning the hospital and find out how June was. It wasn't that I didn't want to know, I intended going to the hospital later that evening but right now I wanted to focus on finding Murray. As it happened the hospital told me nothing, only that June had attended an afternoon therapy session and was comfortable but appeared to be very tired.

Mrs Lawson rapped on the passenger window of the car and startled both Janet and me into a state of fright. We hadn't seen her approach as it was a typical overcast and wet Glasgow day in January. It was two in the afternoon but could have been midnight for all the light there was. I had a brief chuckle as I thought how the Scottish Tourist Board could market Glasgow to vampires worldwide as a winter destination with very short overcast days; they would certainly run a very low risk of being caught in the sunlight.

Mr and Mrs Davidson were delightful and as sharp as a *Gillette Mach 3* fresh from the pack. They regaled us with tales of the dance halls in the fifties. Like the Locarno, the Barrowlands Ballroom and the Plaza. They also admitted to freely indulging in *Red Biddy* a cheap and plentiful fortified red wine, the 1950's equivalent of buckfast. Both Janet and I laughed at the thought of the buckie drinkers of today asking their grandparents about *Red Biddy* and discovering that those grandparents got up to basically the same shenanigans that they were, albeit without the selfie's as evidence of their drunken stupidity.

They did tell us about a few incidents that suggested there may have been a vampire haunting the Gorbals in 1954 and that it may have been killed by one of the Billy boys a notorious Bridgeton gang of the 1930's that still had some devotees in the 1950's. The gang in the 50's didn't reach the levels of notoriety that it had in the 30's but it was still present even if it was only a shadow of its former self. But nothing they told us was of any use to us, it was too long ago and our own exploits had overtaken those that had happened back then. Nevertheless we had spent a very enjoyable afternoon in the company of two people who could give youngsters a quarter of their age a lesson in how to enjoy life. It was strange to think that Mr and Mrs Davidson's heyday had been seventy years previous, the twinkle in their eyes and mischief in their smiles made it seem as though they still had a trick or two left in them.

It was what happened as we were leaving that shocked me and changed my perspective on everything we had been through and everything we would be going through in the near future.

A nurse approached us as we opened the front door to leave, she was a young woman in her late twenties maybe early thirties. She was pretty and reminded me of someone, I wasn't sure who but it would come back to me, somebody on TV perhaps no it wasn't that maybe it was somebody from my distant past but I couldn't think who. I looked again at her and became conscious that I was staring at her like some kind of stalker. With that inquisitive look on her face and the twinkle in her eye I suddenly remembered who she reminded me of and the resemblance was uncanny they could have been sisters, or come to think of it with the years that had passed they could be mother and daughter.

'Excuse me sir, you need to sign out of the visitors book. Health and safety reasons you see if there's a fire we need to know who is in the building and who isn't' she said in a soft English accent, probably Birmingham or somewhere around the Black Country anyway. I continued to look at her closely, which I quickly realised had started to make her uncomfortable.

'I am sorry sweetheart, I know I was staring at you but you remind me of somebody I knew back in the eighties. What's your name?' I asked and then realised she had a name badge on.

'Sarah Duffy' she answered at the same time as I read her badge.

I smiled and said 'Oh so it's not Keenan then?' which was the maiden name of my first wife and that was who this pretty young woman reminded me of.

She smiled hesitantly and with some suspicion 'No, Keenan's my ma's name though'

I took a few seconds to let that sink in, this wasn't possible. I wasn't sure how to continue but Janet obviously realised what I was getting at, so she asked the all-important question.

'Is your mum called Patricia Keenan?'

The girl looked from Janet to me and then back again with a furrowed brow.

'Yes' she answered warily 'Do you know her?'

I smiled at her and said 'I should think so I was married to her thirty odd years ago, only for a very short time but we were married. How is she? Where is she living? Is she back In Scotland?' I fired rapid questions at her.

The young woman looked at me with apprehension written across her face and blew my life apart with her next question and her next answer.

'Are you Thomas Mundell?' she asked. When I nodded she looked me squarely in the eye and said. 'My mum died two years ago, it was breast cancer. Before she did she told me a secret that she had kept from me my whole life. She told me who my father was' I wasn't particularly good at maths; clearly Janet was better than me at counting because she gasped. I smiled stupidly still not understanding what this young woman was saying to me. She clarified what she meant with two little words.

'Hello dad' she said looking at me. I grinned but still didn't understand the joke. I gave the best answer that I could under the circumstances.

'Eh' I said profoundly.

'Tam for an intelligent man you canny half be dense at times. This lovely young woman is telling you that she is your daughter' Janet said as if it was the most natural thing in the world.

I stopped breathing. My mind ceased to function. My legs followed suit and I sat down, fortunately I retained enough of my motor functions to actually sit down on a nearby chair.

'Well, that's not the reaction I expected' Sarah, my daughter said with the most beautiful smile it had ever been my pleasure to see. I still wasn't breathing, I knew that I had to and soon. There was a fair to middling chance that having only just met my daughter, whom I never knew even existed that I was now about to die at her feet. I tried to talk, my mind had a thousand questions my mouth couldn't manage even one. I suppose, to be fair, it's difficult to talk when you have forgotten how to breathe.

'Tam take a deep breath, you have went all purple and your eyes are bulging, if you canny manage a big breath then at least take a couple of wee breaths' Janet said with genuine laughter in her voice and tears in her eyes. 'Tam you lucky lucky bastard you have a daughter'

'And a granddaughter' Sarah said with her own gorgeous laugh and tears in her eyes.

Just when I thought I might start breathing again she went and dropped the granddaughter bomb.

'Jesus Christ, I mean Jesus fuckin Christ' I said looking round to see who I had offended with my blasphemy and foul language combo.

'What do I do? I had no idea you even existed. What do I do? I want to laugh or cry or run around in a circle shouting yippee. I suppose it's too late to hand out cigars. Or hold in you in my arms and say goo-goo gaga. I haven't a clue what to say or what to do. Help me' I managed to blurt out, so she did help me.

She called me dad again and hugged me, which was possibly the sweetest moment of my entire life. In return I burst into tears and cried like a baby. Which probably wasn't the most macho reaction I could have hoped for but Janet must have thought it was okay because the tears were now streaming down her face as well. When I got some sort of control of my emotions I managed to tell Sarah that I had a thousand questions for her and she managed to nod and tell me that she had twice as many. She was finishing her shift in an hour and we agreed to wait outside and give her a lift home.

Her daughter, my granddaughter wasn't at home. Sarah didn't want to spring me on her too quickly, she knew of the probability that I existed but even so it was all going too quickly. I didn't disagree it was better to spend time with Sarah before meeting Patty, my granddaughter who was named after her maternal grandmother. I thought to myself that I would never tire of saying 'my granddaughter'

Irony of ironies it turned out that she had a flat in the Gorbals, one of the new builds that had replaced Queen Elizabeth square. It was just a stone's throw from the pub where I had met her mother and within a couple of hundred yards of where she had been conceived. Sarah explained what her mother had told her about me. That we had been very much in love, very happy and full of plans for the future. Patricia had only just realised that she may be pregnant and had made a doctor's appointment to confirm it. She was imagining scenarios where she would tell me and we would be overjoyed and excited.

Instead, I spoiled all of that with one moment of madness, one slap, a single act of gross stupidity. I had frightened her profoundly. She, more than most people, understood domestic violence; her father had been arrested umpteen times for publicly assaulting her mother. He had spent six months in prison for a particularly vicious assault which resulted in her mother being hospitalised with internal bleeding, which turned out to be a ruptured womb. Leaving her unable to carry any more children, she was twenty four years old at the time.

So when I struck Patricia, all of those memories flooded in and she instantly decided that she would not give me any opportunity to turn into her father. She fled down south to an aunt and uncle who lived somewhere near Birmingham. Patricia resolved to bring Sarah up on her own; her reasoning for this was that if I, the person she loved and thought loved her could hit her then any man could. She had trusted me implicitly and I had let her down. She would not allow another man to get that close ever again, and she didn't. Sarah told me that her mother had occasional boyfriends but none of them had ever met Sarah or stayed at their home.

During the time Sarah told me all of this, I sat silently, unable to defend myself in any way and unwilling to lie. Everything Patricia had told her was the gospel truth. I had no defence, no excuses, and no escape from my guilt.

Sarah noticed this and tried to throw me a lifeline by saying that her mother may have over-reacted, that she could have given me a second chance. I considered this get out of jail free card and almost grabbed at it. But that would have been denying Patricia's reality; the truth was that she couldn't afford to give me a second chance. Her mother gave her father multiple second chances, which in the end resulted in her being a punch bag for twenty years and her father spending as much time inside prison as outside prison. And the truth was who could say how I would have reacted had I got away with that one slap. I was only 21 it could have instilled in me a feeling that I had a right to strike her when she disagreed, we could have ended up like her parents how can I state as a fact that we wouldn't have.

I stopped berating myself inside my head and asked Sarah if she had known her maternal grandparents and the answer was no, apparently they had moved to Wales in the nineties and then on to Spain in 2004, only to then lose touch and basically disappear. I told her that sadly her paternal grandparents had both died relatively young. She would have loved them, they were good people and I am sure they would have loved her.

My father died in a road accident, he was travelling up to Inverness for a Glasgow Rangers football match and a lorry driver lost concentration and killed him in a pathetically stupid and run of the mill collision. My mother died three years later, officially from a heart attack, she was fifty one and a non-smoker who weighed all of eight stone soaking wet. I think she died from a broken heart, although they didn't have the most passionate start to their life together. My dad had fallen in love with my mum and married her to allow her to keep her illegitimate child, me. My mother had accepted his love and the opportunity it gave her with some trepidation. But over their years together she had grown to love the bones of him. In my opinion she never got over his tragic death and just gave up trying to live. He was her life simple as.

So there we were, I had no one to call a family and Patricia had only her daughter. But that wasn't strictly true, Maggie and Janet were my family as were Stevie and Sonny, and I was unsure whether I could involve her in my life to any great extent. In fact I realised that

I couldn't involve her at all, what the hell was I thinking about? Roderick Murray had killed Stevie and threatened to kill everyone who was important to me. This would be like a gift to him; I could almost hear his laugh in my head.

'Sarah this has been great this catching up, listen give me your number and I will give you a call we should get together again soon' I said outwardly nonchalant but panicking inside and stood up to leave.

Janet looked at me with stark disgust, Sarah looked at me as if I had slapped her, the way I had slapped her mother all those years ago. She looked at me again intensely and I avoided eye contact, I couldn't let her get to me, to open up again to her was too dangerous, for her.

'Actually Tam I don't think I will give you my number, I would like you to leave now' she said, probably trying for an angry tone and only managing a hurt one.

Janet looked at me and said 'What the hell are you playing at you bloody moron, this is your daughter, and your granddaughter' she said pointing at a photograph of what looked like a ten year old girl on the wall behind me. I looked away before I could even glance at the photo that would have been enough to break my resolve.

'Janet, I think you need to keep your nose out of my business. Sarah I will be in touch at some point, just let me get used to all this please' I said and left, gesturing at Janet to come with me.

Janet punched me on the shoulder with venom as we walked downstairs to the car. 'Are you absolutely mental Tam, you just blew your chance to have a family. You might never get that chance again'

I stopped at the car and stood face to face with Janet and I held her arms and looked deep into her eyes and said 'think'.

So she looked back into mine for what seemed like an eternity but was probably only ten seconds and I saw the realisation spring into her eyes. She pulled her arms free to raise both hands to her mouth and say 'Oh Christ Tam he will go after them won't he, oh mammy daddy Tam we need to stop him before he finds out about them, oh Jesus Mary and Joseph Tam what are we going to do' she burst into tears as she slowly grasped the reason for my attitude towards Sarah.

'We are going to go to Sonny's and think, I need to get my head round all this' I replied panicking inside.

'Here that's Sarah's number, she gave me it, hold on to it Tam please' she said handing me a tiny slip of paper.

Too much was happening and too quickly my head was spinning I was trying to think in three different directions at the same time. Within the space of a day I had gone from grieving for one of my best friends, a virtual brother, to trying to take in that not only was I a father I was also a grandfather. Now I had to finish Roderick Murray for good I couldn't allow him to discover my secret family, I had only just found them I was not going to lose them.

2015 the end game.

Sonny was hunched over his laptop making notes and chewing on his bottom lip. Maggie was tidying up a house that was already immaculately tidied; she looked on the verge of tears.

'Well, anything?' she asked us before we even got in the door.

Janet looked at me, I suppose for permission to relay our secret. 'Tam has a daughter and a granddaughter' she squealed like some twelve your old girl who had seen Harry Stiles at a bus stop.

Sonny looked up quizzically; Maggie put her hands to her mouth. 'You were only sent out to get info on the 1950's, where did you go, the adoption shop?' Sonny said and went back to his online scouring.

'Was it Patricia?' Maggie asked, I nodded.

'She must have been pregnant when she left, Omfg Tam, why didn't she tell you? That was incredibly selfish of her; you should have known you had a daughter. Well wait until I see her, she will be getting the sharp end of my tongue' Maggie said with some venom.

'Patricia died last year Maggie, she only told Sarah, her daughter, our daughter, about me just before she died' I said 'And no she wasn't selfish, she thought she was protecting herself and her lassie and after what we have been through for the last thirty years it turns out she was right. I dread to think what might have happened to them and what still might if Murray finds out about them. We need to end him and we need to do it tonight. I said looking at Sonny for support.

'I think I know roughly where he is.' Sonny smiled. 'I had a call from Sinead, Stevie's ex, earlier telling me about a few more young people that had gone missing from the homeless place where she works. He seems to be concentrating in the area around the necropolis again, so I researched all the graves and tombs and think I found his likely location'

We had all flinched slightly when Sonny mentioned Stevie in the past tense; it still hit us hard when we were forced to notice his absence. I don't know about the others but there was an anger building up inside me and every time I was made to remember that Stevie was dead, it grew a little stronger.

Sonny paused to let his news sink in 'There's an unmarked grave Tam over in the eastern necropolis, next to the big grey tomb. I think I have found proof that the unmarked grave is the final resting place of Roderick Murray's wife and children. If it is then I think maybe Murray would be set up in the tomb right next to them. I found an article in the Glasgow Herald from around that time.

> Police in the Gorbals area of Glasgow made the grim discovery of the remains of a woman and two children. They are believed to be the family of Roderick Fitzgerald Murray. The infamous Glasgow solicitor hanged earlier this year. Sergeant Leopold Fox advised this reporter that the bodies appeared to have been set upon by animals. They were bloodless and savaged around their necks. A collection has been organised in the parish to ensure a decent Christian burial as no members of the Murray family have come forward to claim the deceased.
> Father Anthony Towers priest of the local Chapel has agreed to inter them in the Southern Necropolis. Police enquiries are continuing apace.

'That's it then that's where he will be' Janet said, looking out at the darkest of January nights. 'Well that's where he will be at dawn but where is he right now?' she said looking at me with unmistakable fear in her eyes.

'He won't be far away; he's toying with us now. He imagines that we are afraid and cowering, hiding from him, scared of his power. He has killed Stevie and imagines that he has broken us, that he can pick us off one by one. We are to be his amusement over the winter nights, he sent those two unfortunate boys last night to taunt us at the window. He will try to make us believe that he is the victor and we are the vanquished' I said.

'That's a pretty speech Tam, maybe the writing skills are coming back. But this arsehole killed Stevie let's go and find him and rip out his heart and eat it in front of him' Maggie said with a hatred in her voice and on her face that I have no wish to hear or see ever again.

'Ok cool' I replied and all four of us laughed as we prepared ourselves to kill or be killed. Maggie had been busy during the day filling vials with holy water and procuring Crucifixes that made one wonder their normal purpose. They were about eight inches high made of wood with a silver body of Christ pinned to them with tiny silver stakes. The bottom part of the cross was slightly pointed. I held mine in my hand and imagined the opportunity to plunge it into the chest of Murray and stare into his eyes as he breathed his final breath. My heart surged with adrenalin and I was determined that vengeance would be mine, this night.

Two things happened simultaneously as we prepared to leave the flat. All four of us were wrapped sufficiently for a Glasgow January evening stroll in a graveyard. My mobile phone rang and there was a crash at the living room window. A bit more than a crash actually the window frame came completely off, flew across the room and virtually exploded against the opposite wall. It also decapitated a plastic ornamental statue of Charlie Chaplin. Who incidentally would have been proud of the facial expression that Sonny had, it conveyed his shock and horror without the need of sound.

My mobile continued to ring, Maggie did exactly the wrong thing and ran to the space where the window had been, so she was first to see the pitiful horrible thing that Stevie had become. She gasped and threw her hands first to her mouth and then she threw them open and said 'Come in'

'No' Janet and Sonny screamed in unison, but it was too late, the thing that had been Stevie was in and so too was Murray who seemed to materialise from nowhere.

Murray pushed Stevie to the floor and laughed 'ya bunch of Fannies, dae ye no' even know that ye canny invite vampires in?' clearly he had been indulging in Ned blood again.

'We need you in so we can end you' Sonny said and stood with a strength that I admired.

'Don't be stupit ya walloper you canny end anybody, you concentrate on shagging the fat bird and don't go aff your nut and get your balls in your haun, big man. It's the leader off I'm after, how's it hingin Tam the bam?' the vampire said turning to me and grinning through blood stained lips 'cos you are a bam aren't you Tam, ah mean whit kind of numpty doesn't have a Scooby that he has a thirty year old lassie?'

My heart sank, my mind went into overdrive. How could he possibly know, did he know where they are what had he done to them?'

I threw myself at him, ignoring my lack of protection. He swatted me aside like a fly; I flew through the air like one too, landing in the lap of the thing that had been my best friend, Stevie. It looked pitifully down at me and opened its mouth to sink its teeth into my exposed neck. For the briefest of seconds I saw a flash of something in its eye, a miniscule beam of light, a flicker, and then a smile.

Suddenly it catapulted me from its lap and stood upright and bellowed 'come oan then, get inty me' it screamed and attacked its fellow vampire Murray.

It was a colossal coming together in the middle of Sonny's living room floor, the walls shook. Sonny's modest 32" Goodman's TV fell off the wall and cracked across the screen. There was a tinkling of glass as ornaments and mirrors fell to the floor. The two vampires were circling each other warily in the middle of the floor. They lunged at each other teeth bared and snarling before drawing back and snarling again when neither could gain an advantage. I gripped Maggie by the arm and dragged her reluctantly away from the action as I left the flat.

I had to find Sarah and Patty and ensure they were safe. I couldn't afford to let Murray know that I was leaving or where I was going. So as guilty as it made me feel I had to sneak away and leave Sonny and Janet to deal with the mayhem in their living room themselves. My priorities had altered; I no longer had the luxury of protecting or even attempting to protect my friends. I had a family to safeguard now, a daughter and a granddaughter to be precise, if in fact they were even still safe.

Maggie threw me the keys to her stupid wee car and said 'come on we need to find your girls'

I threw the keys back at her and replied 'you drive I need to make a telephone call'

My phone had rang at the same time as Maggie had invited the vampire into Sonny's living room. When I checked the missed call register the number that came up meant nothing to me. It was a Glasgow number but not one I recognised. Whatever it was it could wait. I frantically searched through my pockets for the tiny slip of paper that Janet had handed me with Sarah's mobile number on it. I eventually found it after a panic stricken five minutes of searching. It was in the tiny pocket which is above the right hand pocket of my jeans. What the hell was that stupid wee pocket for all it ever did was get in the bloody way. My first call went to voicemail; I left a stupidly panicky message that would mean nothing to her. My next three calls also went to voicemail. My fourth was answered by a young girl.

'Is this my papa' she asked.

Before I could answer the voice of a woman came on the line, 'I told you I didn't want you contacting us and I meant it' she said as the line went dead. I immediately rang back but predictably the call went straight to voicemail.

I grabbed at Maggie's sleeve 'Give me your phone' I said abruptly and rudely.

She looked at me and shook her head 'It's in my pocket' she advised lifting her left elbow and allowing me access to her jacket pocket. 'But I'm sure your daughter isnae daft, if you ring her on that so soon after her hanging up on you she will suss out that you have just borrowed someone's phone. Leave it we will be at her flat in two minutes anyway'

Rightly or wrongly I was determined to ring again. As it happens it was wrongly, on the first ring Sarah answered and shouted 'go away you stupid stupid man' loud enough for Maggie to hear and set her head shaking from side to side again like a nodding bloody dog.

We pulled up at the front door of Sarah's tenement flats. I rushed to the intercom and frantically pressed every buzzer then I stood back and shouted her name up at the windows above me. She came to the window and held her curtains aside but as soon as she saw me she stood back and closed the curtains. Not very subtle but I got the message anyway. The buzzer on the intercom buzzed and I heard a click as the door catch released. I threw open the door and ran up the stairs, Maggie trailed behind me.

A beautiful young lady stood with the door open and her hand out for me to shake it 'my name's Patty' she said and smiled a smile that the memory of which will go with me to my grave. I was transfixed, immobile; I must have looked a fool.

'Oh Patty, what are you like' Sarah said as she opened the door and stood behind her daughter. Maggie had arrived puffing and panting behind me, strangely I hadn't even noticed the six flights of stairs. 'You two had better come in, I suppose' she said and walked inside.

'She means you two' Patty smiled 'I already live here'

I felt very awkward and embarrassed, I had made a massive fuss to get in and now that I was standing in front of them I had no idea what to say. Sarah wasn't in the mood for letting me ease my way in.

'So banging on the door pressing every buzzer and shouting up at random windows, this better be good' she said and folded her arms across her chest.

I am not an expert in body language but she didn't look as if she was ready for a cosy chat. I shuffled my feet.

'Well, what do you want?' she said giving me no time to think at all so I did what I usually do in those circumstances I fabricated a tale.

'I'm sorry but I was stupid earlier today when I left so abruptly, I didn't feel that you deserved to be related to somebody like me. I am not a very good person, I panicked, what can I say?' I waffled.

'Ok I agree with you' she said in a reasonable tone, that suckered me in. 'You aren't a good person in fact you are quite a pathetic person. So now I would like you to stop snivelling and get out of my house. I have no wish to let Patty see how pathetic you are, we lived this long without you, we obviously weren't missing anything now get out' She uncrossed her arms but only so that she could point at the door.

Patty looked at me sadly, she clearly wanted me to put up a defence, I wanted to put up a defence but how could I switch to the truth and say, by the way Sarah a 100 year old vampire might be after you because you are related to me, have a nice day. Aye right. Luckily I had Maggie with me.

'Sarah, you don't know me and there is no reason on earth why you should listen to me. But, for goodness sake don't listen to this bloody idiot.' She smiled at Patty and continued speaking ' and you young lady are you old enough to make your granda and his friend a wee cup of tea, while him and your mum calm down and have a chat'

Patty looked at both Maggie and I with some suspicion, she was a very smart cookie 'I am old enough to make tea, but I am also old enough to know when I am being sent out of the room for adults to talk turkey' she paused and looked at me 'I don't know what to call you yet, I thought it would be papa but your Scottish word granda seems better. So tell me the truth granda, do you need to speak privately to my mum and is it something that I shouldn't hear?' she asked with an open face and an open heart.

'Yes and yes' I said shrugging my shoulders.

She considered 'ok since you didn't give me any bull, I will make a pot of tea, you have ten minutes max' she flounced away happily enough.

Sarah looked at her leaving with a fair amount of justifiable pride on her face and she turned back to me 'Patty is overly generous; you have five minutes' she looked at Maggie and smiled 'Your lady friend clearly loves you but I am struggling with the concept right now so speak'

I didn't know where to start so Maggie rescued me again. 'Sarah someone extremely bad is trying his best to hurt your father and because of that you and Patty are potential targets for him. Your dad thought today that if he stayed away from you then this evil man may not find you, but he found out somehow that you exist. We don't know if he knows where you are but we also don't know that he doesn't' Maggie said with her usual forthright straightforward, tell the truth and shame the devil manner.

'Hurt you why? What have you done?' Sarah asked warily looking directly into my eyes, expecting the truth. I hesitated.

'I can't believe that you would come here to warn me that my daughter and me may be targets and then sit there and try to make up a cover story to save your blushes. Last chance what have you done, tell me before I call the police' she said folding her arms across her chest again as she stood.

'Sit down Sarah please; this is not an easy thing to tell you. In fact it's a completely crazy nightmare of a thing to even begin to tell you. There is a very good chance that you may phone the police and tell them you have a lunatic in your house and you want him removed' I paused looked down at my feet and plunged in feet first 'The man who is trying to kill me, not hurt me, but actually kill me is called Roderick Fitzgerald Murray, he is well over 100 years old and he is a vampire'

I looked up expectantly, imagining the worst but only seeing the incredulous look on her face, I could only imagine what she was thinking. Maggie jumped in 'Sarah don't dismiss this yet, I have the proof in my car on my laptop, I can prove categorically that your father is telling you the truth'

'I don't doubt he thinks he is speaking the truth, why wouldn't he when he has friends like you feeding his fantasies, I want you both to leave now. I will not have my daughter exposed to your lunacy for one second longer. It's enough that she is addicted to *the vampire diaries and Being Human,* without you two convincing her it's all real. I am completely staggered that a couple of mature adults could be this bloody mental...'

I think she had more to say but a crash and a high pitched scream from her kitchen stopped her in mid-sentence. I was quickest on the run and entered the kitchen just in time to see the face disappear from the corner of the window. I had time to think, *'what is it with these guys and appearing at fucking windows, it was getting right on my fucking nerves'*

I grabbed Patty to my chest and soothed her; I put myself between her and the window.

'It's ok sweetheart, it's ok' I said and was stroking her hair.

Sarah did the motherly thing and shrieked 'get away from her you nutcase' and pulled patty from my arms. Understandably Patty burst into tears and ran to what must have been her bedroom and slammed the door.

Sarah turned on me with hatred in her eyes 'She heard your bullshit about vampires and you frightened her you complete loon'

'She saw someone at your kitchen window, so did I' I said plaintively trying to explain.

'Oh my god, you can't stop can you. We are three storeys up, there is no way anyone could be at the bloody window' she screamed at me.

'This guy Murray does this frequently, he thinks it's funny' I said tamely sounding more and more stupid every time I said anything.

'He's telling the truth mum, there was someone at the window, and who is Murray?' Patty said, as she stood at the kitchen door with tear streaks down both sides of her face.

Sarah went to her and held her tight 'Go to bed pet I will be through in two minutes, I just need to see these two out'

Maggie said 'Sarah, keep her here with you and with us. Even if you are right and we are lunatics then there is no harm done, but if you are wrong and you leave her alone in a room and anything happens to her, you will never forgive yourself. Please let me prove this to you, I beg you, your lives are at stake, all of our lives are at stake'

'I hear your sincerity Maggie and clearly you both think this is true but for god's sake wake up to your delusions, neither of you are old enough for dementia so what the hell is going on here?' Sarah asked getting more confused by the second.

'Was that a vampire at the window?' Patty asked, and when silence greeted her question she said 'I thought it was, it looked like one. Is that who Murray is then? Is he the main man, the central vampire?'

'Stop asking stupid questions Patty, there's no such bloody thing as vampires' Sarah said but with less certainty than before.

'I am not scared mum. Vampires aren't scary as long as you have the right weapons vampires are easy to get rid of. The main reason that vampires kill people is because they don't believe that vampires are real until the very last minute. And by that time they are vampire food' Patty said with surety.

'OMG I can't handle any of this, this is so bloody mad, I need a drink' Sarah said walking into the kitchen and opening the fridge door. As she stood upright with a bottle of white wine in her hand she screamed. Not a terrified scream more the type of scream you would hear when someone saw a mouse unexpectedly.

'Is that it?' Sarah asked pointing at the window.

I stood beside her and said 'No it's not Murray, it's one of the Neds he converted weeks ago and uses to keep an eye on us'

Sarah giggled 'he uses neds as his minions? seriously?'

I laughed with her 'yes he does and occasionally when he has had to resort to feeding from one of his Neds he talks like them. It's pure dead mental man' I said in my best Ned impression.

My phone rang again. When I checked the number intending to cut it off I noticed it was the same one from earlier in the evening. I answered it and wished I hadn't. I listened carefully to what was being said and my heart sank.

'It's the hospital, there's been an incident with June, they won't tell me what it is only that it is serious and I need to get there as soon as I can' I told them.

'You need to go Tam she needs you. June is Tam's wife' Maggie explained to Sarah and Patty.

'We all need to go, I am not staying here another minute with that thing hanging about outside my window' Sarah said.

'If we invite it in and kill it, we would be putting it out of its misery and preventing Murray from knowing where we are' Patty suggested nonchalantly.

Sarah gasped 'OMG what are you saying, we can't just kill someone'

'Mum it's not someone it's an empty shell being controlled by the big vampire. It would be crueller to leave it as it is' Patty explained patiently as if she was the mother and Sarah was the childish daughter.

'Sarah, Patty go wait in the corridor, we won't be two minutes, please take these.' Maggie said holding crucifixes on chains out to both of them. She smiled at me 'I always have a couple of spare on me'

Within seconds of Sarah and Patty closing the door behind them Maggie had opened the kitchen window and invited the ned vampire in. it had only the chance to hiss once before I broke the wooden shaft of Sarah's mop across my knee and drove it through the creatures heart. Maggie crossed herself reverently as we watched the thing transform into what looked like a teenage boy at peace. I hugged Maggie and ushered her from the house, we had no time to waste.

As usual when we got to the hospital it took us twenty minutes or more to even find where June was. It transpired that she was in intensive care, suffering from a near fatal blood loss. The nurse who spoke to us explained that the on call consultant was sure that my wife had somehow got a hold of a two pronged fork during the night and stabbed herself in the neck. Because she had two puncture wounds in her neck and had suffered a massive blood loss. Knowing full well what was likely to have happened, I asked the nurse how much mess there had been, there must have been blood everywhere. She patiently explained to me that the consultant also had a theory that my wife had leaned over the wash hand basin or the toilet and allowed the blood to flow out of her neck and then either rinsed it away or flushed it away, because there was very little sign of blood loss anywhere in the room or on her clothes..

'Let me get this straight' I shouted at her 'My wife who is under observation in a psychiatric unit in this hospital. Has somehow in her locked room been able to manage to magic up a two pronged fork, stab herself in the neck losing most of the blood in her body. Which she managed to let pour out of her without leaving a trace anywhere. Then she magically disappeared the two pronged fork, before dragging herself back into the bed even though she was lifeless and bloodless. Is that basically what you are telling me happened here today?'

The nurse looked at me and said with typical Glaswegian gallows humour 'I know when you say it out loud it seems unlikely but what else could it have been, a vampire? This is Glasgow pal not Transylvania' I looked askance at her and she knew she had crossed a line and started backtracking and apologising profusely. I shrugged off her apologies because they really didn't matter, I knew the truth. June had now been infected and could expect to be waking up pretty soon as a vampire. I was struggling to cope with this now, had Patty and Sarah not been standing less than ten feet away I don't know what I might have done. As it was they took priority now. I couldn't save June, she was the latest victim of Murray's evil, but I had to make sure she was the last. He needed to be stopped and I had to stop him.

I wanted to hunt him down and rip him limb from limb. Maggie stopped me from storming off on a wild goose chase whilst I was still in a rage. 'What about June, Tam, we can't leave her like this, we can't' she said. I knew she was right but June was in intensive care, was I supposed to march in there and pull the plug? Or maybe Maggie expected me to pound a stake through June's heart in the middle of the royal infirmary.

'I can't help her Maggie, not right at this minute, I need to concentrate on protecting the living' I said and pushed past her abruptly. She grabbed at my arm 'Tam, don't do this don't leave her to him. The only thing she did was love you, don't abandon her'

'I'm not abandoning her Maggie; you of all people know I would never do that. I will be back to take care of her but I need to stop him. I need to get back to Sonny's pronto. He may still be there' I said loosening her grip on my arm gently.

She nodded her reluctant agreement and left the hospital with Sarah, patty and I. Maggie cast a backwards pitiful glance, I didn't I had no time. Before we even got to the car my mobile rang again it was Sonny's house phone.

It was him, Murray the vampire and he was laughing. 'Three down, four to go' he said smoothly and hung up. I stopped in my tracks, hesitant at first to say anything but I had learned my lesson with

Sarah, only the truth would do. A lesson I had learned many years previously with Maggie.

'It was Murray, he was delighted to tell me that he has killed Janet and Sonny, he said three down four to go, he means us four' I hung my head the blows to my resilience were coming too hard and too fast.

'He probably hasn't, you know' this came from Patty.

'Hasn't what' her mother asked before either Maggie or I could.

'He probably hasn't killed your friends, in fact he probably hasn't touched them. Vampires are very evil, so he would want you to find them dead or if he had turned them into vampires he would want them to take you by surprise. So he was probably lying about harming them just to wreck your head' Patty explained logically. Maggie grabbed for her mobile phone in her bag managing to spill all of the other contents at her feet.

As soon as she managed to get her hands to stop shaking she called Janet's mobile and immediately discovered that patty was absolutely correct. Both Sonny and Janet were safe, after Maggie had relayed this news to us by jumping up and down mouthing the words 'They are okay' she calmed down and let us know that Janet had put an end to Steve's torment. After Murray and Steve had fought, Steve was in a terrible state on Sonny's living room floor. Janet despatched him quickly and painlessly and watched him turn from the ravaged vampire back into the Stevie we had known and loved. She reckoned that Stevie had mouthed the words thank you all at the end, and who am I to disagree with her.

'You could do worse than listen to me sometimes you know, I am a bit of an expert on vampires and werewolves' Patty offered apropos not much.

'I think you might be right sweetheart so what do you think Murray will do next?' I asked with a tired smile.

'I would think he will be at my house waiting for mum and me to return without you and your friends. He probably thinks that you will be away searching for his lair' she said matter of factly; I was beginning to be in awe of my granddaughter. Not only had she grasped what was happening and believed it immediately, she was showing a line of deductive reasoning that I couldn't fault.

'Okay lets test your theory and give him what he wants, you and your mum can go home' I said.

Maggie and Sarah shrieked their protests almost in harmony.

'You can't seriously be going with a ten year old girl's hunches Tam are you crazy?' Maggie asked.

'You aren't seriously thinking that I will allow you to use patty as bait are you? Was Sarah's more than reasonable question.

'Yes and no' I said smugly 'we are going to take patty's expertise on board and no, nobody will be used as bait. We are all going back to your house Sarah, distraught with the news that Janet and Sonny have been destroyed by Murray. Because as my old granda used to say he doesn't know that we know that he doesn't know that we know. Do you know what I mean?' I said and ushered them all towards Maggie's car.

We tried our best not to look around us as we emerged from Maggie's car and walked slowly up the path to her new style tenement building. Patty went into dramatic actress mode and was wailing about her auntie Janet who had been taken from her almost as soon as she had found her. Sarah didn't add to the solemnity of the occasion by giggling at patty's antics. We made it inside before all four of us collapsed with laughter.

Patty (apparently for the first time in her life) volunteered to make everyone tea; Maggie followed her into the kitchen just in case. Which allowed me time to talk to Sarah on my own; I was trying to explain to Sarah that although she was struggling to believe what was happening that it was indeed all real. I was about to tell her my plan which would include me putting my life on the line again, when the living room window blew into the room, precisely as it had done at Sonny's house earlier on.

'He's here' I said and pushed her towards the kitchen door as I rushed towards the opening where the window had been. It wasn't him it was June my poor poor wife who stood defiantly on the window sill and said 'Tam how could you abandon me please help me Tam, save me from him Tam please'

I nodded to her and held my arms open, it was all the invitation she needed. She was on me instantly even before I had time to open the neck of my shirt and display the crucifix hanging there. As I struggled with her Murray stepped gracefully from the window sill into the room. Maggie emerged from the kitchen in the same instant and immediately came to my aid instead of attacking him, which saved my life. She managed to tear June away from me just as she began to sink her teeth into my wrist.

Murray appeared at my shoulder once more he had descended into Nedpseak.

'Hing oan there Tam the sham don't you start beating up another one of your wifes big man you will get a reputation for it so you will'

I turned round quickly crucifix in hand and Murray shrank back hissing, 'Ahm gonny take that thing aff you and stick it right up your arse one of these days Tambo' he hissed with venomous intent. 'And right after that Thomas I am going to inhale the sweet sweet virginal blood of your granddaughter like a vintage port' he said his nedness wearing off.

'I don't understand what exactly you are saying Mister Murray but I know you are an abomination that has threatened my daughter and that I can't allow' Sarah suddenly said emerging from the kitchen with what looked like a wooden tenderising mallet in her hand. At precisely that moment Maggie said 'Burn in hell Murray' and incredibly pulled a water pistol from her handbag and started spraying Murray with what was obviously holy water he made a bee line for the window but I got between him and his escape route and said 'Not this time Roddy' he spun away from me and impaled himself on the kitchen implement Sarah was holding in front of her. It wasn't a tenderising mallet it was a miniature croquet mallet that she had picked up years previously at a flea market just because she liked the silky feel of the polished Ash that it was made of.

The end.

Afterword;

Hi my name is Patty Duffy; my granda let me read this book even though he thought some of it was too old for me. He also said that I could write this afterword thing and tell all you people what happened next. First of all I don't really know what happened to the vampire, well I never actually seen what happened. I am guessing but, that they chopped his head and limbs off and scattered them all over Scotland preferably under running water, which was my suggestion. And since they kept coming into my mum's kitchen that night looking for a bigger knife and a hacksaw, I think my guess was near enough accurate don't you.

Janet and Sonny turned up a wee while later and helped with whatever the grown up's were doing. They are getting married and I am to be a bridesmaid. I get a feeling that my granda and Maggie might marry each other as well, they look at each other very funny all the time.

That's if my granda's wrist gets better soon that is, I noticed he wrote in his book that Maggie saved him from being bitten by June, I am not so sure that she didn't maybe bite him a wee bit he says absolutely definitely not. But he would say that wouldn't he.

Printed in Great Britain
by Amazon